LOVE JOURNEY

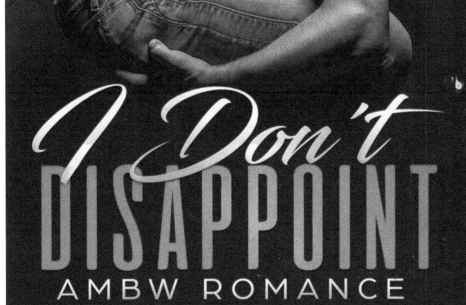

I Don't DISAPPOINT

AMBW ROMANCE

I DON'T DISAPPOINT

AMBW ROMANCE

BY

LOVE JOURNEY

This is a 20k+ word Asian Men Black Women (AMBW) Interracial Erotic Romance. Intended for mature audiences. 18+

DEDICATION

This book is dedicated to all the brown girls around the world that

love Asian men.

Because I know that Asian men love brown girls too.

#AMBWLOVE

BRIEF DESCRIPTION

Daniel Kim is a sexy Korean Hip Hop celebrity at the peak of his fame. He is determined to succeed and has just signed a lucrative contract with a U.S. music label. He's used to sacrificing his happiness for fame and fortune... until he meets Diamond.

Daniel Kim has a 'love jones' for Diamond, and he's feening for her in every way. Physically, mentally... he's all in.

And he promises not to disappoint.

Diamond is a personal photographer assigned to accompany Daniel while he is on a promotional tour. Her job is to photograph, post, and promote the handsome entertainer... not to sleep with him. She's determined to protect her professional reputation even if it means walking away from the best sex she's ever had.

CHAPTER 1

DANIEL

The driver pulled up in front of the SoHo Grand Hotel, and Daniel stepped out of the limousine like a true celebrity he was. Dressed in black jeans and a white designer shirt from his own clothing line, he swaggered under the dark overhang into the hotel lobby, surrounded by his entourage. His black hair was shaved on the sides and perfectly styled into a swooping Mohawk. His signature black shades put the final touch to his look.

The flight from California was lengthy and had turned into one long business meeting as his staff brought him up to date on the plans for their trip. After landing all he wanted to do was check into the hotel, get a bite to eat, and relax. He crossed the lobby with long slow strides, was greeted by the hotel staff, and shown to the registration desk. With a professional smile, his assistant stepped forward to handle the group's reservations. While the details of his stay were being sorted out, he took a brief moment to absorb his surroundings. *Nice.* The hotel lobby was luxurious, with plush chocolate and cream carpeting surrounded by deep rich wood flooring. The hotel offered a plethora of amenities - bars, lounge, pools, and private meeting spaces for guests. But most importantly, they were exclusive and specialized in privacy for their special guests. And as a celebrity, he learned to appreciate that luxury very much.

As he glanced leisurely around the spacious room, a breeze swept across his cheek, drawing his attention to the woman walking through the glass entrance.

Who is that?

CHAPTER 2

DIAMOND

Diamond made her way through the hotel lobby and headed straight to the front desk rolling her bag behind her. Her sunglasses were still resting neatly on her nose, her naturally curly hair touching her shoulders. She had chosen her favorite pair of distressed jeans that hugged her body perfectly with a silver-gray sleeveless top. She could hardly contain her delight as she admired the extravagant interior. Everything was so beautiful.

There was a short wait to check in, so she took the time to people-watch. After taking a mental note of the group of Asian men looking her way, she gave them a quick nod before turning toward the waiting registration clerk. *They're all watching me.* With a pink blush on her cheeks, she quickly moved forward and smiled at the desk clerk.

"Hello, and welcome to the SoHo Grand Hotel. How may I help you?"

"Hello, my name is Diamond Butler, and I have a reservation for one."

"I will be more than happy to help you with that, Ms. Butler," the clerk said, smiling as she made all the necessary arrangements for the room and key. She handed her the keycard and offered an enthusiastic, "Please enjoy your stay!"

"Thank you! I will!" Diamond responded, turning to grab her bags. She felt a strange urge to look to her right. There standing in the middle of the group of Asian men was - *him*. She knew exactly who he was though they had never met. Although he was wearing dark shades, she could feel the heat of his gaze on her. Nervously, she dipped her head and turned to head towards the elevators, knowing that she and he would meet sooner rather than later.

DANIEL

"Woah," Daniel whispered to the guys as the beautiful woman walked away from the reception area. "Who is that?" He tilted his head in her direction. They all turned at once to watch her sway sexily towards the elevators.

"Thicker than a snicker," Brian said.

"More cushion for the pushin," Joshua agreed.

"Mine." *Wait. Where did that come from?*

He must have said it out loud because now his entire group was looking at him strangely, but he didn't care. All his attention was on her.

Her skin was the color of sweet, creamy honey. The fitted material of her gray top complemented her thick figure perfectly, revealing her brown shoulders, accentuating her ample breasts, and falling smoothly around her full hips.

Breathtaking.

He was staring, and he didn't care.

CHAPTER 3

DIAMOND

Diamond loved her job. As a freelance photographer for the stars, celebrities fought her to become their personal paparazzi for photo shoots, filming, interviews, parties, and club appearances. She was highly sought after for one very important reason - her magic camera lens.

She had a talent for capturing a unique side of people.

She had developed a love for photography at an early age after learning to take pictures with her parent's old camera. For years she had developed her technique and enjoyed capturing the smiles of her family and friends, but she really found her calling the summer she worked as an assistant for a wedding photographer. That's when she discovered her unique and mysterious talent to tell a person's "other" story through her lens.

She was a magician behind the lens of a camera.

After completing that internship, she went on to study photojournalism at the Chicago School of the Arts and worked for the Multi-Digital Media Group. Moving on to start a freelance service studio, Diamond grew her niche by hiring out as a personal paparazzi photographer to A-list celebrities for video shoots, events, premieres, and appearances. Her services allowed celebrities the opportunity to exercise a bit of control over their public image.

She got the opportunity to travel to the most beautiful places and meet a variety of celebrities and other people working in the industry. Unknown to most, she preferred to operate in the background. She liked to blend into the crowd and melt into the sidelines. Most of all she liked to see another side of people through the lens of her camera. A softer side, or a crueler one.

Working with celebrities was cool. She discovered that superstars were very much different behind the scenes. When they were not in the public's eye, their softer side came through. And that's why people hired her – to give the public another version of themselves. It was becoming increasingly important to have a good social media presence, and she gave her clients the material to work with.

She knew her stuff.

Fans wanted to see the day to day side of their heroes. And for a short period, they got that from her. From the beginning of a project to the end, she and her camera were there. From morning meals with the crew to the midnight swimming parties - she was always present with her magic box, ready to capture the moment. She liked the candid shots, like when people laughed at a joke or were lost in their own thoughts. Those were the winners.

One drawback to being so close to certain celebrities on a day to day basis was the constant propositions. And she was propositioned a lot. Sometimes male actors, social media stars, musicians, rappers, and other A-list celebs were so used to getting whatever they wanted that they forgot that she was off limits. Before taking on a project, she always made it very clear in writing that she did not date or sleep with her clients. She found that lines could sometimes become very blurry after too much alcohol and nudity.

Her goal was to stay out of the way and give her clients a polished portfolio in the end - period. Remaining professional at all times and never crossing boundaries kept her in business. She was private, very discreet, and never sold secrets. Celebrities could be themselves around her and not have to worry about being given a bad presentation.

Number one rule in the industry - No sexual relationships. Unfortunately, she had once crossed that line a long time ago and paid the price with a broken heart. After that, she vowed with all her soul that it would never happen again. No one else would ever get that close, only to discard her like yesterday's news.

DANIEL

Sexy and controversial. Two words that could be used to describe Korean-American hip-hop star, Daniel Kim. His reputation often preceded him in the music industry, and he didn't give a damn. He was a self-made success, and he had worked harder than anyone to get to where he was today.

Daniel had started out from the bottom and through hard work as a trainee and tireless dedication he had launched his own independent record label and a very successful solo career. Now, five years and four albums later he was quickly becoming an international household name. Without a doubt, the man was sexy, confident, and serious about his business.

In a recent turn of events, he had signed a major deal with ZAP Entertainment as its first Asian American artist. As an international Asian-American singer, songwriter, dancer, record producer, model, and CEO of an independent record label, he was extremely busy. After having laid the groundwork himself, he was ready to hire a team of professionals to handle the day to day business so he could concentrate on making music.

Turning thirty had been an eye opener for him. He loved music, and his career was flourishing, but his personal life had taken a backseat for several years. Many of his childhood friends were getting married and having children, and he hadn't had a solid relationship for years. Being a CEO and artist were two full-time jobs - ones he had given every ounce of his being to. He had a great support system and was surrounded by family, friends, and industry professionals who were very involved, but he was missing that special someone to share his life with.

So after some self-reflection and reevaluation, he had decided to free up some of his time, and finally live a semi-normal life. He wanted to hang out with friends, relax, and make music. And if he happened to meet a special someone along the way he would love to fall in love.

Relationships were hard for him. All he seemed to run across were gold diggers and industry rats. Sadly, women always seemed to come with an agenda - money, and fame. Years ago, he had fallen for a user, and her indiscretions had nearly ended his career. Getting his heart broken and feeling betrayed hurt his creativity and career motivation. He slipped into a depressed slump after finding out that the girl he loved had slept with half the Korean music industry. He had just been another "come up" for her.

So after that experience, he vowed to never be a victim again, and for quite a few years, he played the field.

Pretty girls were his weakness and one night stands became his new claim to fame. Daniel had a reputation as the industry player and pretty boy pussy slayer. He took what he wanted, left them satisfied and moved on. But turning thirty had brought him healing and a calmer look at life. It was time for a change.

And that's how he had come to team up with Blue.

CHAPTER 4

Diamond was a contract photographer for Blue Strategies, a full-service public relations agency specializing in celebrity and event-driven press in the music industry. They were well known for providing high-quality services and creating exciting PR campaigns. After working with Blue, celebrities became leaders on the music scene. They guaranteed professionalism, energy, and fresh ideas. Their clients included a long list of up and coming musicians from around the world.

Blue offered first-class marketing assistance, special event planning, premium social media management, and world-class celebrity endorsements. They employed the industry's top stylists, makeup artists, journalists, photographers, videographers, editors, and event planners. Whatever a celebrity needed to build their social media - Blue provided.

So it was no surprise when Daniel Kim's team reached out to Blue to help promote his new album with a series of summer events. They wanted a full behind the scenes PR team including personal stylist, hair and makeup, location management, and most importantly they needed a personal photographer with him every step of the way.

He had a full schedule of photo shoots, videos, interviews, club appearances, and a red carpet premiere lined up for his one month trip to New York and he wanted only the best.

And that's how he met Diamond.

CHAPTER 5

The hotel conference room was the perfect place to hold a large team meeting. The room was intimate yet spacious, and the floor to ceiling windows created an inviting atmosphere. The cherry wood conference table ran the length of the room, an array of flowers, pastries, and high-end glass water bottles down the center.

At exactly nine, Team Blue and Team Daniel filed into the brightly lit conference room to have breakfast, make introductions, and make sure everyone was on the same page. On one side of the conference table sat the public relations team and on the other were Daniel and his people.

One minute he was biting into a muffin and the next he was frozen in place. Because when she walked into the room time stood still.

Holy shit! That's her?

He sat up straight as her confident steps brought her to a seat directly in front of him – up close and personal.

Uhhhhhhhhhhh

Another woman, with a black business suit, slicked-back bun, and glasses, stood and clinked her fork against her glass to get everyone's attention. After everyone settled down, she began. "Good morning. My name is Denim Montgomery, and I'm your public relations representative with Blue Strategies. Please allow me to introduce my team..."

Thank God for dark sunglasses - because damn!

His imagination was running wild. From his vantage point behind the dark lenses, he couldn't help but stare at the honey-hued woman sitting across from him. She wore a white V-necked sleeveless belted jumpsuit, and her reddish-brown hair was pulled into a cute messy bun on top of her head. He was fascinated by the fact that she only wore eyeliner and pale pink lip gloss on her lips. But more breathtaking was the way the sun brightened when she smiled.

Oh my god, she's beautiful.

His breath caught in his throat as she stood to introduce herself. Rising out of the chair, she blessed them all with the full vision of her curvy frame. *Good, God! She's juicy!* This woman was stacked. Round breasts, full hips, and thick thighs. *She's got curves for days. Damn, I bet she'd feel soft in my arms.*

Looking directly at him with a professional smile she said, "Hello, my name is Diamond, and I will be your personal photographer. I look forward to being a part of your behind the scenes PR team. My job is to capture a different side of you through my lens and help to create the image that you want to present to the world. I will be with you day and night at every event leading up to the premiere. If there is anything specific that you're looking for, please don't hesitate to ask. I'll make it happen."

Gulp. Day and night huh? Well, there goes my 60 days of celibacy.

He felt an elbow in his side and heard someone next to him clear their throat. Quickly, he closed his mouth. Giving her an acknowledging nod, he sat up straighter in his chair and tried to look professional. She noticed the small gesture and blushed before taking her seat.

Two more people spoke after Diamond, but he didn't hear a word. He was distracted by the sound of his racing heart beating hard against his rib cage. To prevent anyone from noticing that his hands were trembling, he removed them from the table top and placed them in his lap. *What the hell is wrong with me? Why do I feel nervous? I'm hiring them, not the other way around.* He stole another glance in her direction. *That's why.*

He looked to the right again when Denim stood again. "Well, that ends all of the introductions. Do you have any questions for me or the team, Mr. Park?"

"As a matter of fact, I would like to go over a few details with..." He motioned toward Diamond.

"You can call me Diamond," she responded with a smile.

"Ah, would that be Mrs. or Ms.?"

The entire room was silent, and everyone was focused on her for a response. She cleared her throat and nervously shifted in her seat before responding, "Ms."

A predatory smile lit up his face as he removed his sunglasses, leaned forward, and looked her directly in the eye, "Perfect," he said leaning forward. "Ms. Diamond, would you care to join me after this meeting for a little one-on-one so we can discuss my photography preferences? There are certain positions... I mean angles that bring out the best in me. And since we will be spending a lot of time together we should probably get to know each other better, right?"

She met his gaze head-on. "As you wish, Mr. Park." *I accept the challenge.*

"Oh, please call me Daniel."

CHAPTER 6

DIAMOND

A hot tub?

The invitation to get wet was completely unexpected. When he asked her to meet him in his hotel suite after the morning meeting, she hadn't expected this, so she collected some equipment and took the elevator up to his penthouse suite. She was used to meeting in hotel rooms and never had a problem conducting business there but wasn't sure how to interpret Daniel's request to join him in the huge hot tub in the middle of the living of his hotel suite.

Daniel gave a lopsided grin. "Care to join me? I don't get many chances to relax so I thought we could talk and soak our muscles at the same time."

"I uh... I'm not prepared."

"Please don't get the wrong idea. It's just that I have been in dance practice every day for two weeks preparing for this video and I'm sore. No one's here so feel free to skinny dip if you like."

"Um...thanks but no thanks. That would be very unprofessional."

"Suit yourself. But if you change your mind I have some extra shirts and shorts that might fit you. You're more than welcome."

Not wanting to offend her new client and start off on a bad footing she came up with an idea. "That's okay." She reached down and started to roll her pants up to her thighs. "If you don't mind I'll just sit right here on the edge and put my feet in." *See that's a great compromise. No harm no foul. Crisis averted.*

He just shrugged and walked toward the hot tub while pulling his shirt over his head.

His tattoos were a beautiful collage of personal art, and covered half of his upper torso and right arm. Back facing her, muscles rippling under his skin like a predatory feline, he stepped into the hot tub.

"Mmm. That feels good." He closed his eyes and slid down into the bubbling water. He sat back and placed his hands along the rim of the tub.

Gulp. She couldn't help but stare. He was lean, fit, and exotic in a way. Daniel had these beautiful eyes that slanted down at the outer corner. His skin was a smooth creamy white, and his lips were full enough to nip between her teeth. *Mmm.* She could tell that he worked out regularly because the man had an out-of-this-world six pack. The kind that made a woman want to slowly run her fingers over its tight waves of muscle.

Wave after delicious wave after delicious wave after...

Someone cleared their throat and pulled her out of her enticing daydream of wet rippling abs suddenly. Quickly she closed her parted lips and tore her gaze from the tempting half-naked man in the hot tub. "Excuse me. I uh…" she was having trouble putting together a coherent thought. "Bathroom… I…." she fumbled with the camera in her hand. "I'll be right back." She ran to the bathroom and shut the door.

Oh shit! Oh shit! Oh shit!

DANIEL

The truth is... I'm glad she left the room because I was sporting a major erection under this water.

Daniel could feel the huge smile on his face as he laid back once again into the relaxing water. The look on her face had been priceless. *So she isn't immune to my charms.* In her daze, her lips had parted, and he had almost come up out of the water after her. She had looked like she needed to be kissed when she pulled her lower lip between her teeth and all he could think about was tasting her sweet lips. But now was not the time. It was just too soon.

But damn if she didn't intrigue him. After noticing her in the hotel lobby and finding out later that she was going to be working closely with him, he had decided to take his time and pursue her cautiously. The last thing he wanted to do was create a tense working relationship over the first few weeks by sleeping with his personal photographer. Not yet at least. Because he knew from the moment, she sat down across the table from him that she was going to be different.

The bathroom door opened and she came out barefoot with her shoes in hand. "I just wanted to wash my feet a little before joining you." *Mmm hmm.* With her pant legs still rolled around her thighs, she walked over to the hot tub and sat on the opposite edge before swinging her legs around. She was directly in front of him, but oh so far away it seemed. *I'll fix that in a few minutes. I have to take it easy with this one.*

"So tell me about yourself, Diamond," he said stretching out in the water.

"Well, I've worked with Blue for seven years, and I have a degree in ..."

"No, no, no... I mean the real Diamond. Your likes and dislikes. What makes you happy?"

Her brows pulled together. "Oh, well... I like photography. I always have and capturing a mysterious side of people through the lens of my camera excites me. What about you?" she asked looking up at him.

He smiled. "I like making music. So I guess that means we're both doing what we love to do, huh?"

"I guess it does." She visibly relaxed and lifted one foot out of the water rolling her ankle before dipping it back below the surface.

French manicured toes. I like.

"My turn again." He sat up straight and lowered his hands under the moving water. "Where do you live?"

"Right now I'm staying in Chicago, but I travel so much the world is my oyster."

"Same here."

"Well, I know you live in California and have a close network of family and friends. I also know you have worked really hard to build your business and brand. I also know that you're a certified ladies' man. All that is in the news." they both laughed. "But I guess I would like to know what you do in your free time? What does Daniel Kim do to unwind?" she tilted her head to the side and looked at him quizzically.

"Great question. I like... I like... Well, hell I'm not sure what I like anymore outside of singing and dancing. It's been so long since I had any free time I don't know what it's like. Today is the first day I have a few hours to myself in a very long time, but tomorrow we'll be back at it again. So I guess I would have to say eating and sleeping is what I wish I could do more of."

"Aww Daniel. That's sad."

He shrugged. "It is what it is. I have a lot of people depending on me, so I do what needs to be done. What about you?"

"I like to eat out."

He mouth dropped open, and then a big-ass smile spread across his face. "For real?" he wagged his eyebrows. "Me too! I would never have pegged you as bisexual though..."

"Nasty... At restaurants! I like to eat out at restaurants!" she screamed with laughter as she flicked water in his direction with her fingertips. "You're so nasty. I should've known your mind would be in the gutter."

The fake look of surprise correlated perfectly with the clenched hand pressed against his chest. "Who me? Hey, I take offense to that...not!" He chuckled as he moved to the center of the hot tub and floated on his back above the water. "You're right. I'm nasty as fuck, but I can guarantee you that I'll be the best you ever had. I don't disappoint."

"Is that right?" She raised an eyebrow. *I knew it was coming.*

While he was floating in in the water, the current had pushed him further in her direction. Without warning, he went underwater and then stood up slowly two feet directly in front of her. The water stopped at his waist and dripped down his toned chest. He took one hand and ran it through his shiny black hair as he locked eyes with her and bit his bottom lip. He knew he looked damn good.

Then he leaned towards her, placed his hands on either side of her hips with his face stopping inches from her own. Eye to eye she met his challenge with a raised brow.

"Diamond, I'll ruin you for other men. Just say the word. I've been imagining sucking on your lips all day."

He held his place, waited for her to make a move, and breathed in her vanilla scent. Most women came easily. All he needed was a touch of her hand, and he was going to wrap her legs around his waist and give her the best ride of her life. It had been two months since he'd felt a woman in his arms and he was aching for some hot wet pussy. He watched her eyes glance at his lips and rise back up. The corner of his mouth lifted into a half grin. *You know you want to kiss me. Here I am, come get me.* His fingers flexed ready to scoop her up.

"Daniel?" she whispered.

"Yes?"

"The word…" she took a deep breath and blew her peppermint breath against his lips. "The word is - no."

The smile dropped from his mouth as all his hot fantasies deflated like a balloon. *Playing hard to get? No problem. I'm a patient man.*

"You sure?" he asked as he broke eye contact and shrugged. "Your loss."

"Probably, but it's for the best."

He carefully fell back into the water. "Really? How so?"

"Daniel, I'm a professional and so are you. I want both of us to have a positive experience while we work together, and throwing sex into the mix is a big no-no in my book. I don't sleep with clients - ever. You're cute and all, but I'm not interested in a one night stand with anyone - no matter how good you are, ha. So I hope that clears the air and we can return to a healthy professional working relationship." She added insult to injury by sticking out her hand for him to shake. He laughed and took her hand in a firm grip. Before letting it go, he made her a promise. "Challenge accepted."

She shook her head and swung her legs out of the water and over the side in order to stand. "No, no, no. That was not a challenge, sir. That was a fact." Grabbing a towel off the stack next to the edge she bent over to dry her legs. "I'm your personal photographer, and I work hard. My job is to fade into the background and capture your beauty through the lens of my camera. So getting back on track, is there anything you don't want me to do in these next two weeks?"

"As a matter of fact, there is... I would like it if you wouldn't bend over in wet cream pants that I can see through and show me a thong I can't pull off with my teeth." he laughed.

She stood up quickly and threw her hands across her backside. "Daniel!"

He just shrugged innocently and sat back in the water. "You might see me naked a couple of times, just keep those pictures to yourself."

She laughed, picked up the camera she brought, and turned to snap a picture of him in the hot tub. "I'll see you tomorrow for the early morning photo shoot."

"Mmm hmm."

DIAMOND

Damn, that was close!

Diamond hadn't thought about her pants becoming transparent. *Oh well.* She hurried down the hall to the elevator. That one-on-one meeting with Daniel taught her two things. First, Daniel was big trouble. And second, it had been way too long since the last time she had sex.

When Daniel had moved in close enough to kiss the temperature in the room had shot up to two hundred degrees. It had been a very long time since someone almost made her forget herself.

She hadn't dated much in the last couple of years. The few dates she had been on had felt more like either business dinners or charity cases. She hadn't found that special person who made her want to throw caution to the wind and take a chance on love. She hadn't even had the faintest interest in a man until now - but Daniel broke through her defenses somehow. There was something about him that took her breath away and left her unable to think clearly.

It didn't make sense. Usually, she was unaffected by her client's advances. Most of the time, she just politely declined their propositions and kindly redirected them to the task at hand. But she had had trouble doing that with Daniel back in his hotel room.

Celibacy is a bitch! My reaction just means that it has been too long. That's all... right?

CHAPTER 7

DIAMOND

The morning of the photoshoot was a hustle and bustle of people, clothing, equipment, and shuttle buses. Three luxury vans with dark-tinted windows were parked in front of the hotel, and all the staff was boarded comfortably. The first two vehicles went ahead to prepare the studio. Diamond stayed behind to accompany Daniel and get some before -pictures.

When she didn't see Daniel downstairs, she went up to his room and knocked on the door.

It swung open, and Daniel stood smiling on the other side in nothing but a white hotel towel wrapped around his waist. "Hey."

She took in the sight of pure sexiness. She had seen earlier pictures of him from years ago when he was thin. But looking at him up close and personal was another story. The years had been good to him, and now he was thick in all the right places.

Her face was flushed. "Good morning. I came to see if you needed help with anything," she greeted.

"Yeah, I'm running a little late. Please come in."

The man was fresh out the shower and smelling good. He opened the door a little further and stood back so she could enter. He was drying his hair with a small towel and smiling as she tried to walk by without touching him. And though she succeeded in not making any kind of skin to skin contact, his scent wrapped around her making her breathe in deep as his natural smell seduced her senses. It was like a mixture of ginger, leather, and Egyptian musk - warm and manly.

He closed the door behind her and walked past her into the room. "The good thing about photo shoots is that I don't have to prepare in advance. They prefer I show up as-is, which saves me time in the morning." He picked up a pair of boxer briefs.

Diamond was stuck in a trance, and her eyes were locked on him. His cologne had triggered something deep within her and hadn't yet let her go. It was familiar yet strange. His own unforgettable personal scent, mixed with trouble and seduction. How unfortunate. She was a sucker for a good smelling man.

"Diamond?"

Her mouth was watering, so she licked her lips. *I wonder if he tastes as good as he smells.*

"Diamond?"

Someone was calling her name, but she couldn't quite pull herself away from the visual fantasy of warm arms pulling her in and that scent devouring her. "Hmm."

"Last chance."

Last chance? "I'm sorry, what? I don't..."

He dropped the towel.

Holy crap!

DANIEL

I warned her.

She had that damn look in her eyes again, like she wanted...no needed him to kiss her. She was biting her lower lip, and her eyes had glazed over with yearning. It didn't help that Daniel was damn near naked with only a towel to cover his growing erection.

Damn, if she keeps looking at me like that we might not make this photoshoot. Well, I'm going to put her to the test by dropping this towel. If she takes one step in my direction, we're going to move this bed all across this room. If she bolts I'll do the right thing and get dressed. One...

"Diamond?"

She's still staring at me. Two...

"Diamond?"

I wonder what she's daydreaming about. Three...

The corners of his mouth turned up. "Last Chance."

Ready or not here I go. Drop... Come and get it if you dare.

She screamed, "Ahhhh! Daniel! Oh my god!" Her eyes went wide before she quickly turned her back to him.

He just chuckled and picked up his black boxer briefs and slid them into place. "To be fair, I did warn you." He laughed again. "When you stare it makes me think you want more than a peek."

"Uh, no. It means hurry up and get dressed, and I'll wait outside." She started to walk towards the door.

"Wait." Without warning, he was standing behind her with his hands on each of her upper arms. She was so close he could smell her fresh, clean scent. *She smells like Japanese Cherry Blossom.* He was so close he could feel her body tremble under his touch. *Man, I don't want to mess this up. Go easy.* He whispered in her ear, "I just wanted to hug you and say good morning." So he wrapped his arms around her, buried his face in her neck, and inhaled. "You smell nice."

Another shiver went through her body. "Daniel, please don't."

He knew his erection was pressing against her backside, but he didn't move his hips against her like his body craved to do. He silently vowed to wait for her to make the first move. "It's just a hug, Diamond. Today is going to be busy and hectic, and I just wanted a quiet moment with you. I can't hug you?"

She let her bags fall to the floor before twisting in his arms to face him. He held his breath when she looked him directly in the eyes. They were standing chest to chest and hip to hip. His arms were loosely around her waist. Up close she was even more beautiful. No makeup. Her thick natural curls were piled into a neat knot on top of her head. Her lips were plump and ready to be...

"No Daniel," she said without moving. "You've got to stop flirting with me. I won't sleep with you for one very good reason."

A corner of his mouth lifted. "And what's that?" he asked.

"I like my job, and I don't sleep with my clients. Ever." She searched his eyes. "Daniel, I need you to respect that."

He heard every word she had to say, but he also felt her heart beating rapidly against his chest. Her mouth was saying one thing, but her body was saying another. In any case, his mother raised him to be a gentleman - and a verbal no meant no.

He loosened his arms but didn't let her go completely. "I respect what you're saying, but I see how you look at me. And I can feel how your body responds to me."

Her expression closed up as she shrugged her shoulders and wiggled out of his embrace. "So?"

Now that took him by surprise. No denial. *Just so?* His eyebrows rose, and he looked perplexed.

"So what? I'm physically attracted to you. No big deal. I'm a grown woman and have excellent self-control." She bent down to retrieve one of her bags. "You're an attractive celebrity for goodness sake. I'm sure you have plenty of women throwing themselves at you, but I won't be another notch on your headboard."

"Ouch. That's not fair." He released her and walked back to the bed. Picking up a shirt he pulled it over his head. "For your information, I've been celibate for two months now." He quickly stuck a leg into his jeans.

Watching him dress was distracting, so she walked to the door and placed her hand on the knob. His last statement stopped her before she twisted the handle. "See! That explains it. You're just horny because this is the longest you've ever gone without sex. Now I get it."

He raised his right eyebrow in response. "Do you?" he asked as he slipped on his socks.

She took a deep breath before answering. "I do." She turned in his direction. "You want to know what it would be like to be with a black girl."

He laughed out loud as he pulled on one shoe. "Nope. I've been with plenty of black girls."

"Okay, you want to know what it's like to be with…"

"You." I looked her directly in the eye. "I want to know what it's like to be with YOU."

She gulped.

No, no, no, no, no. She turned to the door and twisted the handle. "We're late, and people are going to wonder what took so long. We'd better go."

He smiled at her back as he followed her out into the hall.

DIAMOND

The studio space was buzzing with activity. The large old warehouse had been transformed into one giant open blank canvas - excellent for photo shoots. A large screen blanketed a wall at one end of the wide room, and the photography equipment took up the other end. She had worked with most of the people here on several promotional shoots in the past. Hip Hop Giants Magazine was footing the bill for this event in exchange for an exclusive first interview of ZAP Entertainment's first signed Korean-American Hip-Hop entertainer. Diamond was present as a secondary photographer to capture the event overall.

She was talking to Peter, the lighting guy when Daniel finally came out of the dressing room. They had arrived 20 minutes late, but it was nothing unexpected. Celebrities were known to arrive late, so it was customary to add an extra hour to at the beginning of any activity. Diamond was still a little curious after their morning encounter, but as long as they were working, she kept her questions to herself.

Despite having to stick to him like glue, there were times when she wouldn't have to be by his side. At night, when he slept, for example. The plan was to meet early in the morning and then she would follow him around all day. Today was special, though. Today was the first official photo shoot, and Diamond was admittedly excited about it. She was finally going to do the thing she had been hired for. She found that she was much more comfortable looking at Daniel through the lens of her camera, blending into the background was her specialty. Her surroundings were distorted by the blur around the edge of her lens, and she could escape reality for a few moments.

"What's up, Diamond?" Daniel stepped into view, his dark eyes narrowed seductively.

She swallowed.

Daniel was wearing a pair of dark blue designer jeans that rode his hips perfectly. They were a complementary contrast to his creamy tattooed naked chest which was glistening with oil.

Does this man ever wear a shirt?

Though he had let her know previously that he thought she was a beautiful woman, she was determined not to let that affect the quality of her work. She couldn't risk her colleagues thinking she was having an affair with one of her clients so planned to continue to gently push back his advances. One way was to pretend that they didn't have an encounter this morning. Daniel had the reputation of a flirt, so it was not like his behavior was unexpected. She was a confident woman, a solid ten, as her father used to tell her.

"Not much, Daniel. Just preparing for the shoot. Did you sleep well? You have bags under your eyes. Maybe you should pass by makeup before we start the shoot." She reached a hand up so she could slide her thumb under his eye. Someone had stayed up later than he was supposed to. A small frown twisted her lips before she shouted to the makeup artist. "Jess, I'll need you to do some cover up today!" Then she focused back on Daniel. "Daniel, you go with her, and she'll fix that for you. Can't have you looking like you haven't slept for our first photo shoot now, can we?" The corner of her glossy, full lips lifted up revealing pearly whites.

"Ah, you wound me. Am I not pretty enough for you?" He pouted and pinched her chin between his thumb and index finger before pulling away, his intense gaze still locked on her own. She could feel the edge of her cheekbones tingle. Despite trying her best to ignore his advances, it was pretty hard to do so when he looked so irresistible. Still, professionalism prevailed, she shot him down again.

"Makeup, Daniel. Now," she replied authoritatively, though a slight smile was still curling her lips.

Daniel gestured as if he'd been shot through the heart and chuckled. "Yes, mistress."

She watched him walk away, her heart thumping loudly in her chest. She needed to get a little stronger and put a wall between his pleasantries and her emotions, or she might let that influence her work, and that was the last thing she wanted. Sighing heavily, she watched as the head photographer, Bryson, prepped his camera on the stand facing the photo shoot area.

He decided to go with a white background for the shoot. Daniel always wore black and white clothes, and he would most definitely stand out on a blank background.

Once Daniel came back from the makeup, he stepped onto the set to make sure the photographer could make any last minute adjustments. She was snapping a few photos when Bryson called her name.

"Hey, Diamond, can you do me a favor? The model isn't out of makeup yet, and I need to line up the correct lenses for the duo shots. Can you stand in front of Daniel for a minute so I can take some test shots?"

The color drained from Diamond's face as she looked around in surprise, then nodded in agreement. She was not used to being in front of the camera and was more comfortable fading into the background. "Okay."

Daniel was standing in the center of the white canvas, shirtless and legs spread casually. She hesitantly walked toward him. The makeup girl was busy powdering his face as Diamond stood next to him facing the camera.

Bryson called out again. "I need you to stand a little closer. Stand in front of him a little, so we test the shot." Bryson's face disappeared behind the camera. *Click, click.*

Diamond stepped into place, feeling Daniel's body heat behind her. She was trying to compose herself, but she had to admit that the proximity just made things a lot harder. The bright lights and his naked chest were enough to make anyone a nervous wreck. As if sensing her discomfort, Daniel pulled her back into his space, chest to back and his front to her rear. Memories of that morning's embrace danced across her mind, and she forgot where they were for a hot second. *Click, click.*

She turned her face to look up at him in protest but stopped when she met his smiling gaze. *Why do I love it when he smiles?* She couldn't help but relax into his embrace and return his soothing look. *Click, click.*

He winked at her. *Click, click.*

She giggled. *Click, click.*

He held her gaze as he slowly reached up to swipe an imaginary piece of lint from her temple. *Click, click.* The contact was so innocent and brief that her defense faltered for a brief moment.

Click, click.

She looked at him - really took him in. *Click, click.*

His silky black hair was perfectly swept up into a stylish wave. His eyes were the color of smooth dark chocolate with an exotic slant at the outer edges. *A person could get lost in those eyes.*

His nose was straight and held a tiny Diamond stud, barely noticeable, in one nostril. But what made her heart flutter in her chest were his full pink lips. *Was it normal for someone's mouth to be so flushed with color? His smile was out of this world. I don't think I have ever seen teeth so white and straight. Aww, I wonder why he stopped smiling all of a sudden. And why are his lips parted? Shit, that's even worse. I wonder if his lips are as soft as they look?*

Click, click.

Her eyes slowly worked their way back up to his eyes and then she saw it - pure, unadulterated desire.

Click, click, click, click, click, click.

"Holy shit that was hot. We got what we needed! Thanks." Bryson yelled. Then it all came crashing back to reality, and she remembered where she was. Her cheeks turned pink as Daniel released her from his hold. Refusing to meet his eyes again, she walked off stage on shaky legs.

She didn't know what Bryson meant by "hot," but she felt like she needed some ice water after Daniel pulled away to get ready for the shoot. She couldn't help the sigh of relief that escaped her. Her friend Celeste, the makeup artist, moved closer to her and leaned toward her ear.

"That's the opposite of a problem if you want my opinion." The woman chuckled and gave Diamond a conspicuous look.

"Celeste! This is work, you know?" Despite her answer, Diamond was smiling. She and Celeste had known each other for a long time, and she knew her friend was just teasing her.

"Who said you can't mix business and pleasure? Is it in your contract or something?" Celeste snickered and stole a look at Daniel as the lighting guy told him how to position himself, what was his best side and how the light was supposed to hit him.

"I don't know. I mean, he's good looking and all but screwing my client wouldn't be very professional." She objected, eyes following the length of Daniel's body. At that moment, as he listened to Bryson and posed, she had to admit he was really handsome.

"Well girl, his eyes are almost always latched onto you and let me tell you there's nothing professional in the way he looks at you. Come on, if you don't do it, pass him along to me, will you? I wouldn't mind getting to know him better." Both women laughed, and Diamond gently shoved her away because the session was about to begin. Before focusing on the camera, she gave Daniel another glance. He smiled in her direction and winked which made her heart skip a beat. She offered a small smile in turn and hid the blush spreading across her cheeks behind the camera.

Mood music played loudly in the background as Bryson's commanding voice boomed. "Alright. Is everyone ready? Let's start with something simple. Daniel? I want you to look natural. Walk around the X as you normally would and ignore the camera. Pretend you see a beautiful flower on the ground, look up at the sky and shield your eyes from the sun. We'll take a few pictures, then we'll move to our designated location for an outside photo shoot if the weather is in the mood."

The sky was clear with a few white puffy clouds here and there. The sun was shining brightly, and the news predicted a warm afternoon, so hopefully, things would continue smoothly after lunch.

The indoor session was a big success, and by lunchtime, Diamond was back in her professional state of mind. "Good job, everyone! I want you on the Serras Street set in one-hour pronto. Break for lunch!" Bryson gave the direction to the crew and had the assistants pick up the props for the outside photo shoot scheduled in the afternoon. Daniel walked up to her after the chaos settled.

"Do you have a lunch hour too, Diamond?" The way he said her name sounded so intimate.

"Only half of it. I have to prepare for the outside session," she replied matter-of-factly, a small smile curling her lips.

"Can I grab a sandwich with you, then? Maybe I can look at some of your shots?" he said and shrugged casually. A grey and white button down flannel now covered his bare chest.

Her eyes narrowed suspiciously, unsure if he was up to something devious or not.

"I'm eating the chicken salad lunch box if you want one too? I'm sure you don't want anything too heavy before the next naked session." Feeling surprisingly comfortable in his presence, she wagged her eyebrows and laughed.

Daniel laughed out loud. "Oh, you've got jokes. Be careful, I like a woman with a wicked sense of humor." He joined her at the buffet table, grabbed a box, and motioned for her to follow him. "I have a private room upstairs, let's enjoy a little peace and quiet while I look over your shots."

She quietly followed Daniel up the staircase, and they entered a cozy little green room on the second floor. It was comfortably set up with a small kitchenette, couches, a table, and a small shower room in the corner. After closing the door, he plopped down on one of the black couches, exhaling in comfort as he laid back and swung his feet onto the cushions. "Man oh man, I needed a minute off my feet. Whew."

She hadn't had many contracts where the celebrities ate with the help, so she was operating in new territory. Knowing that they didn't have much time before they were expected at the new site, she sat their lunch boxes on the table and walked over to hand Daniel her camera.

He was still lying back, so she bent over to flick through a few pictures on the small review screen. She was talking and pointing to a picture she thought would be a good social media header when she noticed that he was not responding. She looked down and caught him staring at her closely. The faces were so close she could feel the breath from his lips against her cheek. They both were frozen in each other's gaze. His lips parted, and he slowly searched her face. She could feel his stare like a caress against her flushed amber skin. In an effort to break the trance she cleared her throat and pushed the camera into his hands. Their fingers accidentally brushed in the exchange causing her breath to catch in her throat. She jerked away, hoping he hadn't noticed.

Nervously, she pointed to the camera. "Just hit the back button and tell me what you like."

His attention was focused on the review screen. "Sounds easy enough. Feel free to grab a drink from the mini-fridge if you're thirsty."

"Thank you. Do you want something?"

"Water, please. These look good," He clicked the button and turned the camera sideways. "I especially like the close-ups. Your camera makes me look good."

Nope. I'm not touching that one with a ten-foot pole. "Mmm. The chicken salad is good. I love this deli because they put grapes in the recipe." She slid his box over to him. "You should try it."

He sat up and opened the box. Reaching inside he said, "Oh yeah? You better be right, because if not you owe me dinner."

She peered at him and froze with her sandwich halfway to her lips. Thinking it over, she knew she couldn't lose. "You're on!" With a huge grin on her face, she took another bite and vigorously shook her head up and down. "Yum Yum."

He chuckled before bringing the flaky croissant sandwich to his lips and closed his eye as he slowly chewed the first bite. She waited for his analysis.

"Nice." he nodded his head. "Damn I really wanted that dinner. I guess I'll have to try a different way because I'd be lying if I said this wasn't good."

Her entire face lit up with laughter as she rolled her eyes, "You're a mess!"

They finished their lunches and huddled over her camera for the next thirty minutes. They both relaxed laughed, talked, and enjoyed each other's company until it was time to leave.

Once they reached Serras Street, they heard Bryson giving the crew instructions. The setting was ideal, and the sky was clear, revealing a warm, bright sun that would give good lighting to the scene. They were photographing him next to a small bridge, giving him a more serious and raw edge. The goal was to show a street side of Daniel to his public and give him a depth people might not have expected.

"Everyone in position! Let's shoot!" Bryson yelled.

She focused her camera on Daniel as he positioned himself against the railing. Through the lens, she watched him search the crowd until his eyes landed on her. In a gesture far too personal for the photo shoot, his gaze looked past the camera and into her soul.

She snapped several photos of him deliberately pulling his lower lip between his teeth.

Gulp. I might be in trouble.

DANIEL

The photoshoot was a full day event, and everyone was hungry when it was finally over.

He had twisted and held his body in several positions he didn't think were possible before today. And though his body hurt in places he didn't even know existed, he had enjoyed the experience.

Diamond was a joy to work with and be around. She was professional and understood the demands of his career. At lunch, they had talked with such ease that he found himself sad when the hour ended. So when the production manager paid a visit to the set, he asked if he could speak to her privately.

Daniel had an idea to help his efforts of getting to know the cute little photographer a little better, so he pulled Denim to the side for a private meeting about the schedule.

"A private island?"

"Yes, a private island would be the perfect spot for a video shoot and a little rest and relaxation. I need a break and want to look my best for the cameras." He flashed that 200-watt smile he was known for. "A buddy of mine owns a 22-acre private island resort south of Key West. I've never had the opportunity to shoot a video there, and I think this would be a perfect time."

"Hmm...opportune time huh? Don't you mean an opportune place to seduce a pretty little photographer who shall remain nameless?"

His mouth fell open as he faked a look of surprise and placed his hand on his chest, "Who me? Seduce? I would never use a tropical island resort to win the affections of a stubborn woman. Can you believe she said that, Jose?" He elbowed his assistant, who was standing next to him. "I was merely making a business suggestion to a budget-minded production manager who I'm sure would appreciate the idea of a discounted use of an island location."

She looked at him skeptically at first, and then her eyes lifted to the ceiling as she started calculating the savings in her head.

Seeing her interest, he continued, "Privacy, space for everyone, beautiful beaches…" he leaned forward, "and minimal rent."

Her head dropped and pursed her lips. "Okay, but under one condition."

"And what condition is that?"

"Don't hurt her, Daniel."

He started to say something, but Denim raised her hand in the air to silence his protest. Looking at him with concern in her eyes, she spoke softly. "I'm speaking as her friend and not your PR person right now, okay? Diamond is one of my dearest friends, and I would never set her up to be used by anybody, not even you. She is the real deal - genuine, kind, and sweet. She has been hurt before, and it took her a long time to recover, so I'm going to ask you to think twice about trying to sleep with her if you can't commit. She deserves more than a one night stand." After speaking her peace, she stood and extended her hand in his direction. "Deal?"

He stood, shook her hand, and looked her directly in the eye, "Deal."

"Okay, get me the details, and I will send a scout to look at the location ASAP."

"Done. And Denim? I'm not out to hurt her and will consider everything you just said. I appreciate the honesty." He turned to leave the room after handing her the island portfolio packet that he had prepared in advance.

CHAPTER 8

DIAMOND

Later that evening, the entire team gathered for dinner in the hotel conference room and the nightly wrap-up news.

The hotel laid out a beautiful spread of mixed grilled kabobs with shrimp, sirloin, chicken, vegetables, mushrooms, scallops, and pasta.

After everyone was served and settled in their seats, Denim stood and tapped her fork against her empty wine glass. "Attention everyone. Congratulations, on a successful photo shoot today." Everyone clapped and smiled at one another. "I have a special announcement. There has been a change of plans for our next adventure." The room fell silent in anticipation of the unexpected news. "Our next event is changing locations. We're going to Iris Key Island!" the production manager announced with excitement.

The room erupted in cheers as everyone reveled in the exciting news.

Denim continued, "To be more specific, we're combining the video shoot with a little rest and relaxation. Everyone had been working so hard, and Daniel has put in twice the number of hours as his team. So the managers have decided to mix a little business with pleasure on the island of fun. We leave the day after tomorrow for three days total. Please make the necessary arrangements and enjoy your meal."

More excitement rippled across the room. Diamond felt someone watching her and looked up to see Daniel staring at her. He sat quietly with his fingers intertwined in his lap, and somehow she knew this was all in his plan.

Nice move, Daniel. You think trapping me on an island will get you into my pants. Nope. Never. Not going to happen. Gulp...

DIAMOND

Daniel's squad and the production team had flown into the Key West International Airport at 10:00am. Afterward, they chartered a small yacht to carry everyone and all the equipment to Iris Key Island. When they stepped off the ship, they were greeted with a beautiful tropical paradise. The sky was blue, almost turquoise, and so vivid that it seemed to be glowing. The palm trees swayed in the breeze, doing their own hula dance.

Paradise.

The flowers, exotic plants she didn't know the name of, were the color of fire; red, oranges with splashes of golds and yellow. She could almost taste the salty ocean air.

Diamond took a deep breath of island air and smiled. The island's owner had hired a friendly staff to help unload and escort everyone to their sleeping quarters. As they disembarked, the staff greeted everyone with a wave and bright smiles with the occasional "Welcome to Iris Island."

She and her luggage were loaded onto a stylish golf cart and whisked off down a path circling the island. She was given a brief tour before being dropped off at her sleeping quarters. The island was shaped like a large teardrop, round at one end and narrowing to a point on the other. Sprinkled with large palm trees and tropical flowers, the landscaping was meticulously manicured. Wide sugar sand beaches circled the entire rim of the island. There was a long walking path down the center that led from one end to the other, with smaller paths that branched off and led to each of the small private villas.

The brightly painted villas were strategically scattered along the shoreline, each with its own unobstructed view of the beautiful blue ocean. In the center of a lush garden was an open-air great hall beautifully decorated with white wicker lounge furniture and whirling ceiling fans. It too offered a 210-degree view of the sparkling ocean waters. The intricate kitchen bar displayed bowls of colorful fruits and vegetables.

This was truly an island paradise.

The golf cart pulled to a stop in front of a buttercup yellow villa with a white wooden wraparound porch. "The villa on the right is yours," the gentleman driver said.

"The right?"

"Yes, ma'am. It's a double. Two connected villas. Another guest will be staying on the other side. Please allow me to help you take your things inside," he said.

Before she could respond a male voice called out. "That's okay. I got it." Daniel walked out of the adjoining villa and down the steps in her direction. "Hey, neighbor." He smiled from ear to ear.

Her mouth fell open as she watched him reach into the back of the cart and lift out her largest bag. She finally got her feet moving, exited the vehicle, and unloaded her other suitcases. "Thank you for helping me. So, you're staying next door? I wonder how that happened." Her eyes sparkled with laughter.

"Have a nice stay, Miss," the driver said before pulling away.

She waved goodbye and lifted her camera equipment case up the stairs toward her quarters.

Daniel returned. "I got it," he said as he grabbed it from her hands and motioned for her to precede him inside the elegantly carved door. When she walked inside the view took her breath away. The cozy room held a magnificent ornate four-poster bed. The white bedding looked wonderfully soft and fluffy. But beyond the downy bed was an awe-inspiring view of an endless stretch of ocean blue.

She couldn't look away from the view. "It's so pretty," she whispered walking towards the covered outdoor veranda. As she stood leaning against the wooden rail looking out across the water, Daniel came up behind her.

"Almost as beautiful as you."

There was a certain hesitation in her eyes, and no matter what she felt, she couldn't help the butterflies dancing her stomach. It wasn't helping that they were in such a romantic setting. The sound of the ocean waves washed over the beach, and the sunlight sparkled around them creating a hypnotizing atmosphere. She felt a quiver of vulnerability.

"Daniel, I honestly don't know what you see in me." She whispered one of the many threads of doubt in her head.

He didn't respond, only took a step closer and seized the rare opportunity. His hands rose to her cheeks, lightly touching them. There was an unasked question in his eyes. Maybe she really wanted this deep down, but the weight of her professional conscience was hard to ignore.

He closed the distance between them and swept her into his arms.

He pressed his lips to her temple, then upon the dark arch of her brow. Each cheek received their share, but Daniel didn't grace her lips with a kiss.

She opened her mouth to speak. He silenced her protest with a kiss. His sensual lips felt soft, like a promise that had long been waiting to be fulfilled.

"Beautiful," he whispered against her lips, warm palms pressed against her cheeks.

Her puckered lips parted when she felt his tongue tracing their outline. A shiver traveled down her spine in anticipation of him breaching the opening. But he moved slowly and savored the mounting desire. Her eyes flew open when he sucked on her top lip, sending a bolt of electricity between her legs. A soft moan escaped her throat as her eyes fluttered closed in ecstasy.

She melted into his embrace, and he lost himself in her kiss. Slender arms wrapped around his neck while he pulled her body tighter against his own. They were closer than they could ever be, trapped in the allure that was their kiss.

Her body ignited with an internal heat as their tongues danced, explored, and teased each other. Their breathing came harder and faster with every nibble, suck, and plunge until she shook in his arms.

Bam, bam, bam. "Daniel! Are you in there?" Somewhere in the distance, someone was knocking on a door.

In surprise, she jumped out of his arms, not wanting to be caught in such a precarious position by their colleagues. *What have I done?* Her hand flew to her mouth, and a look of guilt crossed her face before she raced back inside her villa. Why didn't she see that coming? She really hadn't expected him to do that. She was flattered, out of breath, flustered and angry because she felt like she should have seen it coming or at least stopped him.

DANIEL

Left behind, Daniel stood still on the veranda and drew his bottom lip into his mouth - savoring the lingering flavor of Diamond on his lips.

"Daniel! Are you back here?" his assistant, Jose, called as he rounded the corner to the back of the villa. "There you are. We need to run through the choreography for tomorrow's shoot."

He rolled his eyes and took a deep breath to help steady his racing pulse. "Your timing is horrible, man. Damn!"

Jose looked around, saw no one, and shrugged his shoulders. "You don't look busy to me."

"Sometimes, looks can be deceiving," he said as he descended the porch steps.

Kissing Diamond felt like coming home. She may not know it yet, but I hope that is the last first kiss I ever have.

CHAPTER 9

DIAMOND

Taking advantage of the free time and beautiful weather, Diamond decided to spend time on one of the island's pristine beaches. So, she slipped her feet into a pair of flip-flops and grabbed her camera.

Everyone was busy, so she had the area all to herself. Diamond wiggled her toes in the sand as she overlooked the bluish-green ocean water surrounding the island.

Picture perfect.

She decided to take a few beach photos. She was finalizing the last touches with her zoom when she saw Daniel mysteriously appear through the lens.

What the... A surprised gasp escaped her. She gave him a dirty look and felt like throwing something at him for scaring her so badly.

Fortunately, she didn't have anything, or he would have been in deep trouble.

"Don't scare me like that!" Diamond snapped, one hand grabbing her chest.

"What, now you think I'm scary?"

He took a step forward and closed the distance between them. Again, his eyes felt predatory on her and Diamond had to suppress the shiver that rushed down her spine. *Why did he have to look so good?* His Colgate-worthy smile and the little dimples in his cheeks were far too cute to resist.

DANIEL

Diamond looked like a cool glass of water on a hot summer day. She was standing on a small pristine beach in a coral sundress the stopped at her knees. The way she looked against the backdrop of the ocean took his breath away, so he couldn't resist going to her.

It was early evening, and the sun dipped low in the sky. The soft, warm light, the caressing breeze, all worked together to create an air of romance.

"Let's start back over, okay? I'm sorry. I didn't mean to scare you. Do you mind if I join you? It's peaceful here." Daniel asked.

She took a deep breath and dropped her shoulders. "Sure. No problem. I guess this would be as good a time as any to snap a few photos without any distractions." She lifted the camera in his direction. "May I?"

"Only on one condition."

"Oh, and what would that be?" She zoomed in on his face.

He looked serious. "I want to see what I look like through your eyes. The man inside the star."

Click.

That was deep, and she was curious what the results would be. "Challenge accepted." She knew what needed to be done to get the photos he was asking for and chose to dive right it. "Daniel, what do you want most out of life?"

He turned toward the water and looked out toward the horizon.

Click.

"I want the same thing that other people want - love and happiness. I desire love for my family and friends. I also want happiness for everyone around me, including myself." He nodded his head. "I used to sacrifice myself for everyone else's happiness – but not any longer," he said. "You see, in my culture, we're taught that sacrifice for the greater good is honorable and part of our responsibility to society."

Click.

He continued. "I finally figured out that I deserve happiness too."

Click.

He looked in her direction with a long unfulfilled yearning in his eyes.

Click. Click.

She slowly lowered the camera and looked at him like it was her first time. She walked over to him, looked into his eyes, and said, "I finally see you. Thank you for sharing yourself with me."

They stood that way for a moment, seeing each other in a different way, before turning back to the ocean and watching the waves roll across the water.

That evening, they sat in the warm sand and talked about their lives, hopes, and dreams. They shared each other's fears and disappointments without reservation as they strolled back to their villa hand in hand. And the golden glow of the setting sun had never been more perfect than when he kissed her cheek and bid her goodnight at her door.

On one side of the wall, Daniel stared at the ceiling. Sleep was hard to come by that night as visions of Diamond danced through his head. But little did he know that on the other side of the wall, Diamond hugged a pillow to her chest as she thought about him throughout the night.

CHAPTER 10

DIAMOND

The next day everyone was up early and rushing to prepare for the video shoot. The forecast called for clear skies until late afternoon, after that there was a high chance of rain and lightning.

Diamond and Daniel had spent a lot of time glued together lately, and she'd found a lot of things she liked about him. The way he looked at her made her shiver, but most importantly, he took her seriously. Most industry people she worked with snubbed her profession, referring to her work as a hobby.

Daniel recognized the work she put behind every picture and every shoot. He watched her work the late hours along with everyone else, just to make sure she caught a picture of him at the right moment. Despite how tired she was, she remained alert and ready to snap the moment that would have them both gaining popularity. Already, her pictures were circling the Internet and people were commenting on how amazing the shots were. This couldn't just be a question of taking the right angle and pressing a button, and he gave her that credit, which many hadn't before.

He made her feel special. She was grateful for his acknowledgment but wary. Diamond needed to get her head straight if she didn't want to fall for this famous playboy. The more time she spent with him, the harder it was to resist. She had already slipped once and kissed him, but she couldn't afford to let it happen again.

Men like him do damage to women like me.

She was pulled from her distracting thoughts by the loud voice of the video producer. "Pete, this won't do. The lighting is bad, it gives him a washed out look. Add more lights to the left and maybe a red filter to give a warmer feel to the scene. We don't want cold, pornographic. We want warm, welcoming, and sexy. Okay?"

The video was for his upcoming single, "Beautiful." The concept was great, and the island was the perfect setting for the laid-back side of Daniel and his friends. The song was about a young man who fell in love but had to give it away for his career. She had gone over the song with him, and though most of it was fiction, he was acting it out like a professional. Maybe he should have envisioned a career in cinema too. It seemed like Daniel was a man of many talents.

She was doing her job and stayed out the way snapping photos when Daniel called her to his dressing tent to ask her opinion about his clothing choice. He held up two pairs of pants - one yellow and the other black.

"Where is the rest?" She asked.

The corner of his mouth lifted into a smile. "This is it. What color does your photographer's eye suggest?" Her mouth fell open as he set the pants aside and proceeded to lift his shirt above his head. She couldn't help but stare at his flawless chest up close and personal.

Oh shit.

He gleamed at her wide-eyed expression, puffed out his chest, and flexed his pecs.

"Do you ever wear a shirt?"

He busted out laughing and pulled her into a playful hug. "You're too much."

She stayed in his arms but didn't return the hug right away. She could feel the tension in her body from the effort of holding back. So she inhaled deeply. Her face was right in his neck, and he smelled so good. Oh god, she didn't trust herself. The heat from his skin burned into her cheek. Her eyes closed as she breathed him in one last time.

"Daniel?" Her hands raised and rested on his waist.

He stopped laughing and stroked her back. "Hmm."

"We can't. Someone might come in." She gently pushed at his stomach, taking the opportunity to "accidentally" run her fingers over his washboard abs. *I've wanted to touch these since the hot tub.*

He pulled her in tighter.

"I don't have a problem with that." He looked down into eyes. She looked up into his. "I want you, and I know you want me," he said moving in for a kiss.

There is no way I'm falling into this man's trap of seduction. No, no, no. She closed her eyes and took a deep breath. "Daniel, please don't. Not here. I'm..." His fingers were rubbing deep circles into her lower back causing her to forget what she was saying.

She was so focused on the magic his fingers were working into her flesh that when he pressed a soft kiss to her forehead, she melted against him. The heat building inside of her wanted to take this one chance.

He exhaled heavily. "Diamond?"

She was lost in his touch, but now it was her turn to come back to reality. "Hmm."

"I know I'm going to regret this, but baby I'm barely hanging on here. You feel so good that we might not make it out of this tent anytime soon if we keep this up."

She understood him, and her eyes flew open. "Whoa." She wiggled out of his grasp. "I'm so sorry, I..." she stuttered, and she backed out of the tent. Her steps were swift as she walked in the opposite direction of all the people scrambling around.

DANIEL

Damn.

She'd left him breathless and out of control once again.

That woman is going to be the death of me. Whew. Is it me or is it hot as hell in this tent? He closed his eyes and took in a long slow breath to help ease the tightness of his pants. At that moment he noticed the odd sensation of his heart beating wildly in his chest. His palms were sweaty and his mouth twisted into a lopsided grin.

Uh oh. This was much deeper than just sexual attraction.

He stared at the tent opening and realized that he wanted her desperately. He had never had to work this hard for a woman's affection. But for Diamond, he made every effort to hold back because she was worth it. Besides the fun was in the chase, right?

Continuing to undress, he envisioned the feel of Diamond in his arms. And happiness swept over him.

Daniel chose the black shorts, pulled back the tent flap, and walked out. The glowing sun hit his bare chest, and the ocean breeze cooled his skin. He pulled on his designer shades and scanned the crowd for Diamond.

Spotting her hot pink sundress standing near his group of friends, he walked over to break her away from his flirtatious crew. "What's going on over here? Are you guys trying to steal my girl?"

Everyone laughed and shook hands with friendly familiarity.

Pulling her to the side, he whispered in her ear. "People are waiting for me on set, so I have to go, but I want to talk to you alone after the shoot. There's something I need to tell you."

DIAMOND

Confused, she stammered a small, confused yes and nodded her head before watching him walk away. When it was show time, she sat by the video director and watched intently as the music started and Daniel sang along. The scene they were filming today was with him, his friends and a group of young ladies playing beach volleyball. Throughout the game, Daniel was supposed to lip-sync the lyrics while looking into the camera.

"Stop, stop. This doesn't work. Your eyes, I want them on my camera. I don't know what's on the left, but you need to stop looking that way it makes you look cross-eyed." The director complained, and she realized that she was on the left of the director and the center camera.

"We'll start from the beginning, alright? Don't stress. It's going to be fine." He gestured for the show to roll and the music started again. Stunned, Diamond stayed seated there and just as expected, 30 seconds later they had to stop again for the same reason. Quietly, she moved next to the center camera as they started again, pretending she wanted to see the angle and make sure it wasn't a technical mistake. It was a good cover up because they let her stay behind the camera instead of Johnny, the man who had been designated to capture the center camera angle.

And just as she predicted, Daniel looked straight at the camera this time. The first scene was recorded easily and pocketed after only three more takes for details that bothered the director, but none were linked to Daniel looking left. She could feel her cheeks redden behind the camera because she knew it meant that he was looking at her this whole time while singing. Were the lyrics something he felt? She started to wonder if he really liked her or if he was just teasing her again.

The dancers for the second scene got on stage, most of who were wearing next to nothing. She felt a bit envious looking at all these young women dancing around him, but she knew it was his job. The second verse came in, and he talked about how his life was extravagant, how he could've any women he wanted, but then a dancer moved away from the group, and he focused on her. The lyrics talked about the one, and only he kept thinking about, and Daniel's eyes turned to her again.

"No, no, no! You have to keep looking at your partner. Stop everything! This time you need to focus on the dancer. Move closer, grab her hips, and let her roll her hips against you. Be sexy! We want sensual and romantic, remember? If you keep looking at the camera, the viewer will be as detached as you are of your love story! You need to be more believable!" She couldn't help the chuckle, and the director turned toward her.

"Something funny, Diamond?" His frown deepened. She was walking on eggshells.

"No, I apologize. I just thought that maybe the viewers might think he's looking at them through the camera, but you're the professional here. So..." Diamond started but was quickly interrupted.

"You're the photographer, and I'm the director, honey. I don't need your suggestions but if you can't stay serious while on set, why don't you go fetch us some coffee, huh?"

His reply came as a shock, and she felt it like a slap in the face. Her eyes widened a little, but she was professional, so she didn't say anything about his rudeness. She was used to men trying to shove her back 'into her place,' and it wasn't the first time she had been treated like an assistant.

"Well, if you don't need me, I'll be waiting in the lodge. I'll let your assistant know that you want coffee." She bowed her head politely, gave a glance at Daniel and walked out of the room, humiliated. While she managed to keep her composure and professionalism, it didn't shave anything off her embarrassment. Once she was safely back at the lodge, she downed a bottle of water to calm her nerves.

Minutes later, Daniel was walking in. Apparently, the director's little outburst had soured the mood, and he demanded a short break. Daniel laid into the director next, and filming came to a halt.

With a serious expression, Daniel grabbed her shoulders and closely examined her face, "Are you alright? Don't listen to that ass, you were right, but he wasn't going to hear it. It's my fault for being easily distracted, and I feel like you took a hit meant for me. Want me to fire him?" He caressed her arm, and she chuckled before taking a sip of her bottled water.

She shook her head. She was still irritated but didn't want Daniel to have any problems. "Don't. He might be a chauvinist ass who feels like his masculinity is threatened because there are women on set, but he's good at what he does. It's nothing my pride can't handle, I assure you." Diamond replied and smiled softly at him. To think that he was coming to her defense like a shining knight on a white horse was quite flattering.

"I'm so sorry that you had to suffer because I couldn't keep my eyes off of you. I tried, but the lyrics hit close to home and I couldn't help myself. He's an idiot for not figuring out who I was watching." He leaned forward and kissed her forehead.

She felt herself leaning into his soft lips. "Thank you, Daniel, but really…"

He looked her directly in the eye and said, "No, it's not okay. I don't like the idea of having anyone treat you that way, not on my watch. I know I can't apologize for him but-"

"Daniel, its fine." She was a bit more authoritative with that one. He had a video to shoot and couldn't let his frustrations seep through. "Remember, you need to stay sexy. Angry is not sexy." They chuckled together, and he hugged her close. She felt her heart hammering in her chest and didn't know what to do. When he slowly started to pull away, he gazed deeply into her eyes and replaced a wild strand of brown curly hair behind her ear.

"You really are good for me," he murmured, and before she knew it, his mouth came down on hers. All her self-control went out the door. It was too much. She had never been so weak for another person like this before. His lips were full of passion, devouring and heated, and she was absorbing all his energy.

Someone cleared their throat behind them, but for once she didn't care.

They slowed the kiss to a stop, but he continued to hold her in his arms until they could regain control of their breathing together. His hands flattened on her back. Forehead to forehead they breathed in and out in tandem, taking in each other's breath. The air whispered the words they couldn't say.

Her eyes were still closed, "You have to go."

He whispered back, "I know."

She smiled, "You gotta let go first."

"Never."

"Tonight."

He searched her eyes, and a huge grin broke across his face. "Hell yes." And with that he reluctantly released her body and slipped his hand into hers, giving it a squeeze. Pulling her in for a last minute whisper into her ear, "I don't disappoint. I'm going to make you call my name all night," he said for her ears only.

She took a deep breath to calm her nerves, not that it mattered. On an island, there was nowhere to hide.

CHAPTER 11

DIAMOND

That night thunder and lightning sounded outside the window. She pulled the covers over her head and tried to wish away her sexual frustration.

Damn that man.

Visions of him kissing her replayed in her mind over and over again.

Damn that man.

She was deep into her erotic fantasy and tangled in the sheets when some part of her felt the mattress sag, felt a body slip under the covers. She was about to lash out when she caught his savory scent drifting into her nose, and she knew it was Daniel.

She felt the bright heat of his body push up against her back. His arms wrapped around her waist and his face pressed against the nape of her neck. Her body involuntarily relaxed against him after realizing that she wasn't being assaulted by a stranger in the middle of the night.

Just Daniel.

Before she could say anything, before she could tell him to leave, his lips moved against her skin causing liquid heat to flood her core.

"Diamond."

Afraid of her weak response, she stayed silent. She squeezed her eyes shut and tried to make her body calm down, but it didn't work. His breath was warm as he nuzzled her neck. When she felt his hand caress down her side, her body turned traitor as a low moan escaped her throat against her will.

I must resist.

When she tried to roll away from him, his arms tightened, and he wrapped a leg around her. She felt him grind his generous erection into her backside as a deep moan sounded in his throat.

Oh shit.

Her body ignited into a thousand flames.

Whispering in her ear, he said, "I need you so bad."

He latched onto her neck from the back and licked a trail toward her shoulder. He bit lightly on the smooth brown skin.

He heard her gasp.

Meanwhile, his hand found its way to cup and gently squeeze her plump breast. As he latched onto her shoulder and sucked, he gently rolled a nipple between her fingers. Her entire body backed up into him.

"I can't wait any longer, Diamond. Please don't tell me no. I need to be inside of you."

With an experienced hand, he rolled her onto her back, climbed between her legs, and leaned over her. Searching her eyes, he asked, "Can I make love to you, Diamond? You haven't said no, but I need to be sure."

Her thighs were wrapped around his waist, and she could feel his erection pressed against the junction between her thighs. Her body was on fire, and he could see it in her eyes, so she quickly turned her head to the side to avoid his gaze. *Damn him.*

He didn't move, but she could feel the pulse of his erection beating against her entrance through her panties - begging for permission to enter her folds.

It was becoming harder and harder to hold back, but he was a gentleman and wouldn't force himself on any woman. He knew that her body was saying yes, but he needed to hear the words from her lips. "Diamond, if you want me to stop, I will, but I know you want me just as much as I want you."

He kissed the cheek she presented to him. "Say yes."

He ran his tongue slowly along her jawline. "Please say yes."

He touched his lips gently to the corner of her mouth and whispered, "Oh god please say yes. Put me out of my misery and let me make love to you. All I can think about is you. When I sleep, I see you in my dreams. When I eat, I wonder if you're hungry. I don't even want to tell you what happens in the shower... or maybe I will." He runs his teeth from one side of her chin to the other as she instinctively moves her mouth toward his lips. "When I'm naked in the shower I imagine that it's your hand instead of mine stroking my..."

Her eyes closed and her lips parted in a gasp.

"Shit Diamond. Shit."

He came undone at the sound of her sensual gasp, and he slid his entire body against hers to devour her mouth in a searing kiss. His arms wrapped around the back of her neck and waist and pulled her into his hungry embrace. She desperately threw her arms around his neck as their kiss exploded.

Their bodies moved against each other, desperately seeking release from the other through their layer of clothes. She'd been holding back so long that she felt a familiar tingle flutter in her middle. She pulled back from the kiss, breathing hard, and whispered into his mouth, "Daniel. Please. I'm so close."

He drew her top lip in between his teeth as he stopped all movement, "Say yes, and I'll take you there, over..." he pecked her lips, "...and over..." he moved his hips, "...and over again."

She placed her hands on either side of his face, pulled his forehead to rest against hers, and said between clenched teeth, "Yes," staring him directly in his eyes, "I need you inside me."

Without hesitation, he pushed himself up onto his knees and lifted his shirt over his head. After throwing his shirt onto the floor over the side of the bed, he looked down at her and paused to give her one last chance to change her mind. His upper body was all muscles and tattoos - so sexy - and she couldn't resist lifting a hand and running two fingers over his six pack. His eyes blazed with need as he drew his lower lip between his teeth and watched her slender fingers stroke his skin. "I love it when you touch me."

He is gorgeous. Oh, how she had imagined running her hands over his chiseled abs and beautiful tattoos for days now. Every time he took off his shirt, which was quite often, this very thought ran through her mind. "Your skin is so soft," she said, watching his stomach flex at her touch.

Then a switch flipped. "Shirt. Off. Now," he said as he reached for the hem of her shirt. He helped her raise it over her head, and finally, he was presented with the two most perfect breasts he had ever seen. They were round and full with large dark nipples that had hardened into perfect pacifiers. But before he indulged he pulled off his pants and underwear and tossed them to the floor. He heard her inhale loudly.

"Oh, my." She was checking out his package with obvious approval.

He couldn't help the shy smile that crept up his face in response before he hooked his fingers into either side of her panties and slid them down her thighs. To help him, she lifted both her legs straight into the air, and he slid them past her ankles and past her feet.

They were both completely naked.

He took one of her feet from where it hung in the air and brought her toes to his lips - sucking each one.

Oh. My. Unnn.

He slid his tongue down the bottom of her foot and maneuvered to kiss the inside of her ankle.

Oh shit.

He held her foot in his hand as he kissed and licked up the inside of her calf. Her brows drew together, and her lips parted in response to the sensation of his mouth moving up her leg.

Then he bent and slid his body down on the bed as his lips and tongue kissed a trail up her inner thigh. In response, her back arched off the bed.

Unable to resist, he spread her legs wide open and buried his face between her thighs. Both hands gripped her generous ass while he purposefully wiggled his tongue from her entrance to her clitoris and back again - tasting her sweet wetness on his tongue.

Overwhelmed with pleasure, her head fell back against the bed while biting her lower lip. *Fuck.* She was already close to orgasm from him kissing her earlier. But when he took her clitoris into his mouth and sucked hard, her body started to shake under her building orgasm. "Please don't stop."

Hearing her pleas, he latched onto to her sensitive bud and flicked his tongue repeatedly until he felt her entire body stiffen and vibrate. With a loud cry of ecstasy her body bucked and spasmed as an intense orgasm radiated through her entire body. Stars exploded in her sight.

As her body slowly recovered from the mind-blowing climax, he moved up her body swiftly and pressed his lips against her mouth. His erection was kissing at her entrance, desperately needing to tuck itself inside her warmth. She instinctively wrapped her brown thighs around his hips as he leaned over her. And he easily found her access but resisted the urge to plunge deep. Instead, he raised himself on one elbow and looked deeply into her eyes. Gently, he reached up with the other hand and wiped a strand of hair from her face, then dipped his head to take her mouth in a long deep kiss.

Her hands rubbed his shoulders, neck, and back as he tasted her sweet mouth.

DANIEL

For Daniel, the moment was perfect.

He had imagined Diamond in his arms many times since they started working together. Now he was lying between her thighs and feeling like he had finally made it home. This was a moment to be savored.

While he gazed into her eyes, he moved his hips forward just an inch and felt her body squeeze the tip of his manhood. The sensation of her vaginal grasp caught him by surprise and sent a bolt of electricity into his groin. His mouth fell open from the sensation. "Stop that."

Her eyes danced with mischief as she cocked her head slightly to the side and whispered: "Stop what?"

She did it again.

"You're driving me crazy, Diamond."

She was so slick with moisture that he was no longer able to resist sliding into place with one long slow push.

Through clenched teeth, he groaned, "Oh my god, you feel so good."

"Daniel!" she breathed as he drove forward again, pushing even deeper. He pushed his hands underneath her arms, cupped her shoulders, buried his face in her neck, and ground his hips into her.

"Oh, please DO NOT stop!" she cried.

He was buried deep in her wetness, and a smile spread across his face. *Fuck yes! She's so perfect.*

He pushed deep again and ground the head of his erection into her cervix, sending a tingle down her spine. He pulled out and repeated the grinding motion again, this time making her toes curl. *Fuck.* Her legs started shaking, and her cries grew louder as he wrapped himself around her and rotated his hips in slow circles.

All at once, her eye flew open as another orgasm swept through her body in deep trembles. Taking the cue, he pulled back and let the tip of his erection slide up over her clitoris and watched as her head fell back and a cry escaped her lips.

So wet.

He slid the length of his erection across her sensitive nub and back to the entrance of her weeping hole repeatedly until she screamed his name barely able to recover before another orgasm ripped through her body.

My name never sounded so sweet.

He lost himself as he plunged hard and deep into her silkiness. They fit like a hand and glove. His body on her body. Her mouth on his mouth. Heart to heart.

"I can't believe that I'm coming again! Daniel please!" she cried.

"Me too. Come for me, Diamond," He said as he hit that special spot driving her over the edge once again.

He felt her body tense as her walls drenched him with her wetness. That was it - his breaking point. His body exploded inside of her as he made the final plunge. His orgasm started in the pit of his stomach and spread throughout his body like a volcanic eruption. He was trying not to put all his weight on her, but his arms and legs were drained of energy. He had never cum so hard in his entire life. It was like she sucked the life out of his body, or maybe he poured everything he had into hers. All he knew is that this was different in the best way imaginable and he wanted more.

Later, much later.

He couldn't keep his eyes open one moment longer, so with his last ounce of strength he cupped her in his arms and rolled to the side. And there they stayed, breathing hard and covered in a sheen of sweat, as sleep overcame them both.

CHAPTER 12

DIAMOND

The next morning.

She woke up skin to skin with a very warm body and strong arms. She snuggled in closer and felt his lips on the back of her neck. Flashbacks of their night together put a smile on her face. She had never known sex could be like that. She was on fire, and he was like lightning, burning her to the core.

As soon as he touched her, she fell and crashed into his arms. They created the perfect storm. Now that she knew being with him could be like this, how could she ever resist?

She turned her head slightly and whispered, "Wow."

DANIEL

"More like oh wow," He chuckled deeply in her ear. "I've been waiting on you for like ten minutes."

"Waiting for what?"

He pressed his hardness against her rear. "For this."

A new kind of heat pooled between her thighs when she felt the firmness of his need.

"I've been looking forward to waking up next with you. Mmmmm," he whispered into her ear as he smoothly slipped one of his legs between hers to gently part her thighs.

She liked that idea - a lot. "Well, don't let me stop you." she stretched into him.

His free hand traveled down to slip between her legs and slipped a finger between her folds. With experienced fingers, he circled his wet finger over her sensitive nub. Her mouth opened, pulling in a deep gasp of air.

"That feels so good."

"I know what will feel even better," he responded, gently pushing her forward onto her stomach. Under the covers, they laid chest to back with his face buried in her neck. With one knee he spread her thighs open for his arrival. His erection found its home on its own.

She was so wet and ready for him that his mouth fell open from the sensation of sliding into her folds. Her vaginal walls sucked at him, pulling him further into her moist embrace. It amazed him how perfectly her body responded to his touch.

Instinctively, she lifted her butt to give him deeper access. He couldn't help but squeeze his eye shut and bite his lower lip between his teeth. Nothing had ever felt more right in his entire life than being inside of this woman. Her heat, softness, wetness, moans, and whispers all called to his soul. Unable to resist the magic she was weaving around him, he pressed forward to bury himself deeper in her spell.

His heart knocked against his chest. *Love.*

DIAMOND

Oh, he is squeezing me so tight!

All his hugging, squeezing, and biting was sending her over the edge. With a sense of urgency, she moved underneath him to his rhythm.

"Please..." She squeezed her eyes shut.

"Please don't..." Something big was building in her core with every stroke.

"Please don't stop." She couldn't stop the explosion that moved through her body and out each limb in waves. "Shiiiiiiitttttt."

Daniel wasn't far behind as his body took over and he moved in desperation. He had her locked into place with his feet wrapped around her legs and his arm cupped around her shoulders. His eyes were closed, and a groan escaped his throat as he pounded into convulsing flesh. Their bodies had taken over, and she took everything he had to give. It felt so amazing. He was moving at just the right speed, with the right force, and into the exact right place because her one long, intense orgasm never stopped until she heard him cry out in ecstasy.

He came and came, "Damn, it won't stop! I'm still coming! Ahh!"

Over and over again, "Shit, damn, what the fuck... Ahh!"

He shivered and shook as she milked his body for everything it was worth. "What the hell did you do to me?" he said as he struggled to pull air into his lungs. One last electric shock pulsed down his spine before he collapsed out of exhaustion.

Satisfaction glowed in her eyes as she accepted his weight and drifted off to la la land in his embrace.

The next day back in New York...

CHAPTER 13

DANIEL & DIAMOND

Everything worked out wonderfully! The photo and video shoot receiving their final edits and were scheduled to be released in time for the premiere party. And to top it all off, both teams were well rested from their island vacation and ready to get back to work.

Daniel and Diamond had yet to discuss their romantic interlude. After waking up late the next day, their afternoon quickly dissolved into a mad dash to catch the boat back to the Key West Airport.

It was quickly back to reality for them both.

DIAMOND

Once they arrived in New York, it was back to business as usual. For weeks Daniel was extremely busy preparing for his upcoming stage performance at the red carpet premiere. Their days and night were filled with dance rehearsal, costume design, interviews, and special appearances all over town. Radio stations, television shows, and clubs - she was with him every step of the way. Outside of being his personal photographer, she also managed his social media accounts, distributed information to the press, promoted his brand, and helped him present the best image possible to the public.

Throughout the whirlwind of activities, she tried to keep things platonic and professional but found herself easily distracted whenever he was in her vicinity. Their intimacy evolved into a brush of the shoulder here, a whisper in her ear there, and flirty winks that made her blush from head to toe. Despite her best attempts to remain professional, she couldn't stop thinking about the look in his eyes when he held her and the passionate way he kissed her. It was so intense, so sudden... and she realized that it was much more than sex.

She had connected with Daniel on a much deeper level.

They hadn't been alone since the island. So the night before the premiere, after much debate, she decided to secretly pay a surprise visit to his room.

Down the hall from his room she stopped dead in her tracks. *Why is Denim coming out of Daniel's room? What the hell?*

She could feel the blood rushing to her brain and hear it pumping in her ears. She tried to stop the hammering of her heart as she stood watching Denim share a laugh with Daniel in his doorway.

I should have known. Why am I standing here looking stupid? I should walk away before they notice I'm here.

But her feet weren't doing what her brain commanded them to do. She was in physical shock and unable to move. She felt a small tear begin in her heart, followed by the heat of jealousy. Then, just as her feet were finally starting to receive the "walk away" signal, Denim looked in her direction and …. smiled?

Well hell.

"Diamond? You're just the person I needed to see." She waved for Jason to follow her as she walked in her direction.

I bet I was. She forced a fake smile and looked at Daniel.

Daniel stepped into the hallway with his eyes glued to the floor.

The coward won't even make eye contact with me. She crossed her arms.

Denim looked serious. "We've got a problem."

Uh huh.

They huddled around her, Denim with an "I need something from you" look on her face.

"What's going on?" Diamond asked, switching into business mode and momentarily putting her jealousy to the side.

Diamond gave Daniel, who had an odd smirk on his face, the once over then looked back to Denim, who said, "You see, Daniel is in a predicament. He called me as soon as he got the call. His date for the premiere canceled and no one else is available on such short notice. Daniel was poker-faced.

Diamond's hand fell to her side. *Oh, that's why she was in Daniel's room.*

"As you know, this is a very important day for Daniel..." Denim explained as her forehead furrowed.

Diamond immediately started problem-solving. "Wow, the premiere is tomorrow. I wonder who we can get to stand in at the last minute..."

"...and he can't show up without a date..." Denim continued.

Daniel remained silent.

Unaware of the trap in the works, Diamond looked up at the ceiling in thought. "I'm sure we can think of someone..."

"Oh, we already have!"

"Great! Who?"

Denim and Daniel stared directly at her, giving her time to come to the same conclusion they already had.

Why are they both looking at me so strangely? Wait! What?

Slowly she realized they were referring to her as the replacement. "Nooooooo..."

"Yeeeeessss! I need you to be Daniel's date tonight." Denim announced. Relieved that they had finally breached the subject as planned.

"But...I can't do it. Who's going to take pictures if I wear a dress, stilettos and prance around on his arm?"

But Daniel's partner in crime offered a grin.

"Don't worry about taking pictures, there will be at the very least a hundred photographers on site. I'm sure there will be a few shots taken."

"But I have nothing to wear, and I'm not famous enough to be good publicity for him!"

"But Daniel needs you. You wouldn't let him down, Diamond, right? You're too professional for that."

He chuckled, and Diamond rolled her eyes at him. He knew he had her anyway, it's not like she could say no. She had never walked the red carpet with a celebrity. She was always on the other side of the rope taking photos. But this was for Daniel's career, it would be good for him to be seen with a woman here and there. It would feed the journalists. She knew it. A good celebrity is one we talk about. She just wasn't sure she wanted to be in the middle of that. She rather liked her peaceful and private life. If she did go with him, she might have to give interviews and talk about details of her relationship with Daniel.

"Well, I guess it's settled, then. We have everything taken care of, and the hotel spa is ready and waiting. Hair, nails, dress, shoes... it's all covered. What do you say?"

Diamond glanced in Daniel's direction, and he stuck his bottom lip out in a pout for good measure. There was something about the glint in his eye that let her know some of this theatrical performance was pre-planned.

She crossed her arms and narrowed her eyes at both of them. Through clenched teeth, she agreed. "Fine, I'll go."

Daniel reached forward and lifted the back of Diamond's hand to his lips. His eyes never left hers as he spoke for the first time during the entire exchange, "Thank you, beautiful. I knew I could count on you." Then he winked, causing any reservations she may have had to melt away.

DIAMOND

The next morning was a blur of activity.

She had never been primped, preened, groped, waxed, shaved, scrubbed, steamed, or examined so much in her entire life. The hotel spa staff left nothing untouched - absolutely nothing!

If this is what celebrities go through on a daily basis, they can keep it.

The team had chosen a long sparkling champagne fitted gown with a thigh-high split to reveal her flawless honeyed leg. The expensive material hugged her curvy figure in all the right places. The color complimented her brown skin tone in a striking way, but the way her cleavage was revealed made her a little uncomfortable. She was proud of her curvy figure on any day but wasn't used to showing so much of it.

In the end, it was all worth it. During her fashionably late descent down the hotel's grand staircase to meet Daniel, she swore she saw his jaw drop.

DANIEL

Yeah, I did it. I set the whole thing up. So sue me.

Daniel just couldn't imagine anyone else on his arm for his big night. Diamond was who he wanted to share this moment with, so he had called Denim to put his plan into action. He knew Diamond was too stubborn to agree without a fight, so he did what he felt he had to do.

Now she was walking toward him looking delicious. He liked champagne. *Damn, she looks good enough to eat tonight. Note to self - eat Diamond tonight.*

"Beautiful," he whispered, noticing her cheeks turn pink. Her dress was gorgeous and shimmered down her body with each step she took. Her heels twinkled in the lights like champagne diamonds. Her hair was styled into a sophisticated chiffon bun fit for royalty, and her makeup was minimal but elegant. Her full lips looked delectable, topped off with a bold Risqué Red lipstick.

Yum.

"You're absolutely... I mean you're..." He was looking for his words, and Diamond couldn't help but blush. "You're like a dream."

Not the word she thought he would say. Beautiful, maybe. Gorgeous, likely. Like a dream? This seemed to be a compliment that went past just her physical exterior. Glowing, she accepted Daniel's arm in an elegant manner.

"You look very handsome. You know I'm surprised that you're wearing a shirt. Your tux is another kind of sexy on you."

Another laugh escaped him. "If you look at me that way when I do, I'll make sure to wear them more often."

Thump. Thump, thump, thump. His heart skipped a beat when she laughed.

"Ah... uh. Let's go." Her face was flushed, and she looked nervous, but Daniel washed away all her fears when he took her hand and walked with her to the limousine that whisked them away to the premiere.

Once they were inside the car alone, he gazed turned heated. She reached a hand to his face, caressed his cheek gently, and felt his face lean into her palm. She reluctantly pulled it away. They were not out on a date. They were not out on a date. She repeated these words in her head a couple time just to remind herself that tonight, she was just arm candy.

They arrived at the premiere. Daniel exited the limousine first and turned to offer her his hand in a grand sweeping gesture. Once on the red carpet, the number of flashes made her a little dizzy, but Daniel's hand was firm, and he quickly wrapped an arm around her shoulder. She kept smiling as she had been instructed to do and once inside the building, offered her hand to whoever Daniel was meeting.

This event was more glamorous than anything she had ever seen. She had been a photographer for years and had covered many red carpet events but attending as a guest was a first for her. Daniel was in his element.

She was very proud of how well he worked the media and crowd with ease. The cameras loved him.

So, when a microphone was shoved into her face, she was a little startled. "So how does it feel to be here with the ultra-famous Daniel Kim on the night of his premiere?" A video camera light blinded her.

Did they think she was a novice? *Think again, honey.* Without skipping a beat, she plastered a smile on her face and said, "I'm so happy for Daniel. He has worked so hard to get here. I have never met a man who deserves success more than Daniel Kim."

"Really? Why?" The reporter asked interested in her response.

"Daniel is a professional. He shows up early and leaves late. He works just as hard and right alongside his team. Not only is he a talented artist, but he is passionate about making music."

"So are you Daniel's new love interest?" the reporter asked anxious to be the first to break the exciting news.

"I...um..." she hesitated, unsure how to answer.

Just in time, a hand slipped around her waist, and she looked up into Daniel's smiling eyes. He winked before his mouth came down on hers. All the cameras seemed to disappear as he pulled her against him. Her eyes closed and she leaned into him. He answered the reporter's question, and Diamond's too, as he pressed his mouth to hers - saying all the things he had never said out loud. There was no pretense, only clarity.

There were hand claps and whistles in the background. He slowly ended the kiss and placed his forehead against hers. With a searching look into her eyes, he asked a very loaded question with one word, "Yes?"

She smiled and whispered, "Yes."

Still holding her in his arms, he turned to the camera and smiled brightly. "Did you hear that? She said yes! Sorry, no more questions. I need to celebrate with my future wife." He intertwined his fingers with hers and whisked her away.

CHAPTER 14

DANIEL & DIAMOND

After dinner, all the guests were brought together for a special debut of Daniel Kim's latest album and music video on the big screen. The show was amazing and included fireworks and several artist tributes. The highlight of the evening came when ZAP Entertainment welcomed Daniel to the family and congratulated him as their first Asian American artist to sign a ten million dollar deal.

Daniel was making history and Diamond was right by his side.

As the evening came to a close, both of them were absolutely drained, but happy. A lot of work had gone into this final production, and everyone deserved some time to celebrate their accomplishments.

Leaving together, Daniel offered Diamond a nightcap once they made it back to the hotel. As she closed and locked the door from the inside, she knew there would be more than a celebratory drink tonight. The way he looked at her as he presented her with a glass of champagne from his personal bar was telltale of his wicked intentions... and she couldn't find it in herself to disappoint.

Feeling mischievous, she sipped her drink extra slowly just to make him wait a little longer. *A little delayed gratification never hurt anyone.*

He was standing directly in front of her looking tempting as ever. Taking a final sip, he licked his lips and set his glass to the side. Then he reached for her glass, and she playfully moved it out of his grasp.

"I think I forgot to congratulate you on all your achievements this evening," she said with an impish grin.

Recognizing her game he silently accepted her challenge with a raised brow. Before she knew what was happening he had used the nearby remote control to turn the stereo system to a slow sensual tune. Then he unbuttoned his suit jacket. While holding her gaze, he peeled it off his shoulders and tossed it into the chair. "I think you did twice already."

"Oh," she said, trying to think of another way to carry out her plan to tease him. "Well, maybe you're hungry. Should I call for room service?"

"What I want to eat is already here. Didn't I tell you? That was the plan from the moment you walked down those stairs looking delicious."

She gulped.

He took a predatory step in her direction and captured her glass. Her knees knocked against each other in surrender.

Holding her eyes, he proceeded to slowly remove every item of clothing he was wearing. Mesmerized, she found that it quite difficult to resist a fine ass naked man standing directly within her grasp.

"Wh... What are you doing?" She asked, almost breathless.

"If you have to ask, I might need to try a different direction," he said, and then walked behind her.

She felt his hand slowly unzip the back of her dress then slip it from her shoulders. The material fell in a puddle around her feet.

"Um Um Um."

She knew he was referring to her other secret weapon. She was wearing a cream thong and strapless bra set. And she could tell the string was buried deep between her generous cheeks.

"I like what I see. Leave the heels on, for now."

Wetness pooled between her legs as he stood skin to skin behind her. His hand reached around her body and cupped one breast in each hand. She couldn't help but melt back into him as he kneaded her nipples between his fingers.

"Ahhhhh," she moaned as he worked his magic. She felt him push her forward with his body toward the mint green sitting armchair by the window.

"Listen carefully. I want you to face the chair and place one knee on one arm and the other knee on the other."

It took some maneuvering, but she got up onto the chair's arms, on her knees. They were wide cushioned arms, so the position was pretty comfortable. Her hands were holding onto the back of the chair to help her stay in place. The next thing she knew, he had slid into a sitting position in the chair. Her breasts, stomach, and throbbing core were right in his face. *Oh.*

"Dinner time. Try not to fall okay," he said with a devilish wink. He sank lower into the chair, moved her thong to the side, and exposed her to his gaze. Without hesitation, he took one long lick of her clitoris, causing her to jump. She couldn't move left, right, up or down and was completely at his mercy.

Suddenly he sucked her sensitive nub into his mouth slurping loudly. Stars raced across her vision, and a squeal sounded from her throat. "Ah."

Letting go with a pop and smacking his lips, he circled her clitoris and her hungry vaginal opening in a torturous figure eight. Up, down, and around... over and over again until her knees shook. In the next breath, he pushed his tongue into her opening and let her ride his tongue.

He had two hands full of her ass as she circled her hips on his mouth. Then his tongue went straight up to devour her pulsing nub again. He briefly released her and said, "I know you're almost there. Come on, give it to me." His lips grabbed on again and sucked hard. She nearly collapsed with the force of her orgasm. Her body shook and convulsed as he pulled her down into his embrace as he held her through it.

As her body slowly stopped twitching, he flipped them around in the chair, so she was sitting in it. He pulled her hips down to the edge of the seat. Standing above her he placed her thighs on each of his shoulders and thrust into her wetness. She gulped for air.

He was so deep inside her she felt him in her stomach.

Bam, bam, bam.

He was thrusting in and out of her, faster and faster, and she felt desperate for every stroke.

"Yes! Yes! Yes!" She took everything he had to give.

"I'm sorry. You just make me so...." he closed his eyes in ecstasy. "Oh fuck." His mouth fell open.

Suddenly he looked her in the eye. "Come on we're going to bed." He let one leg down to the floor and held the other in the crook of his arm. He stood them both up still buried deep in her folds, and half carried her, hopping on one leg to the bed.

They fell onto the mattress together, quickly picking up where they left off. She lifted her knees around him as he buried himself inside her over and over again. He was licking and sucking her neck, making her lose control.

Her hands rubbed all over his body, and she sank her teeth into his collarbone as she came again. Daniel loved to see her cum and took pleasure in being the source of that pleasure. But she wanted to please him as well, so she latched onto his neck with her mouth and flicked her tongue over his sensitive flesh. He lost it.

She met him thrust for thrust. He held on for dear life as he slammed into her with his first orgasm. Daniel screamed and moaned as his life force flowed from his body into hers.

"I love you! God, I love you!" he declared, and then collapsed. They laid there in each other's arms as his heart raced along with hers.

Pum pum.

Pum pum.

Pum pum.

Shaking and barely able to lift his head, he looked through her eyes into her soul.

Pum pum.

Pum pum.

Pum pum.

The look in her eyes matched his own, without either of them saying a

word. He pressed his lips to her forehead searching.

Pum pum.

Pum pum.

Pum pum.

He breathed her in. Waiting.

Pum pum.

Pum pum.

Pum pum.

He kissed each of her eye lids tenderly.

Pum pum.

Pum pum.

His heart slowed as he reached for her lips in a loving, tender kiss. They were still joined together, not knowing where he began or she ended. Not wanting to let go.

Pum pum.

Pum pum.

Pum pum.

Slowly he began to move his hips against her again - reigniting the fire. In the heat of passion, he had staked his claim and laid his heart on the line. And at his most vulnerable moment, he looked her in the eye and asked, "Yes?"

She looked at him tenderly, put her hand over his heart, and simply said, "A thousand times - yes."

THE END

I hope you found this worthy of a 5-star review.

Good reviews help me tremendously.

Thank you for reading!

A SPECIAL BONUS JUST FOR YOU!

What more AMBW romance?

Turn the page for a glimpse into *Saved By The Chase*

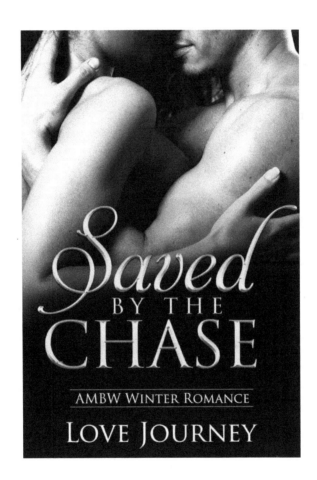

DESCRIPTION

Actor and singer, Hyun-Li had lost everything because he had broken up with the wrong woman. His ex-girlfriend took everything from him - his career, his reputation, millions of dollars, and his peace of mind. Now she wanted his life.

How will he escape?

Good Samaritan, Monique, can't stand by while a man is almost killed. So when she sees Hyun-Li lying on the ground bleeding, she takes a chance to save him. But with a blizzard headed their way and a group of mercenaries on their tale, will they survive? Will they escape …. Will the chase lead Hyun-Li to love?

If you love steamy Asian Men Black Women (AMBW) Interracial Romance novellas, then you'll love *Saved By The Chase* by Love Journey.

SAVED BY THE CHASE

CHAPTER 1

Every South Korean news headlines read "Kim Hyun-Li Cleared of Charges Brought by Ex."

I sat in my lawyer's office and breathed a sigh of relief. "Finally! Maybe now everyone will get off my back," I had been battling my ex-girlfriend in court for the last two years, and I was exhausted. I should have believed her when she vowed to ruin me if I ever left her.

She did just that.

In the beginning, we had lived a passionate whirlwind love affair. I had been head-over-heels in love with her, and she hid her certifiably psychotic tendencies. *Why don't people come with an "I'm crazy" label when you meet them?*

We went from vacationing around the world as Korea's next power couple to battling very publicly in court. Her psychotic behavior began after I moved out of our Seoul downtown condo. After numerous fights and months of non-stop arguing, I just couldn't take the screaming and flying dishes anymore. I had done my fair share of yelling, and the stress was beginning to take its toll on my health and career. So I got out while I could.

She vowed to ruin my life.

But I never imagined she would take me through so much public drama as a result of our split. As a recording artist and A-list actor in South Korea, I had worked hard for many years to earn my fame. And for the last two years, she had made every attempt to take it all away. First, she sued me for assault and demanded a public apology. After the media crucified me and my career started going down the drain, my legal team suggested I settle the suit with the public apology she demanded. It was humiliating, mostly because it wasn't true. She had posted fake pictures of bruises, and the news outlets ate it up.

I lost so many sponsors and movie deals that I settled the court case and apologized for something that never happened. After all that, she called me crying and asked for my forgiveness. She said she couldn't live without me and didn't know of any other way to get my attention.

"You just left! You wouldn't even talk to me! What was I supposed to do? I love you! I felt like I would die without you! Please allow me to apologize in person. I just want to make things right," she pleaded over the phone.

And I did.

Wrong move. She brought wine, that I still believe was spiked, and seduced me. When I woke up the next morning, she was in my bed, and I had a horrible headache. But even worse was that there was no condom in sight. Before the day ended she threatened to take her own life if I didn't come back to her. We had been down that road so many times in the past, and I just wasn't willing to get sucked into the emotional blackmail again. I told her that we shouldn't see each other anymore and that really pissed her off. She said she would make me pay, as she stormed out of my apartment.

And she did.

One month later, she claimed she was pregnant by me and sued me for emotional distress from an earlier pregnancy with me.

What earlier pregnancy! There was no pregnancy!

Oh but the media had a field day with her latest claims and my parents were even dragged into the legal mess.

I wish I had never met her!

But it was too late. Even though I had counter-sued her and won a defamation of character lawsuit, my career was irreparable, and I might not ever work in the entertainment industry again.

She had taken everything - my career, my reputation, millions of dollars, my peace of mind, and now the joy of my first child. I lost it all because I had broken up with the leader of the Korean Mafia's daughter.

And to make matter's worse, she was determined to use my first child

to make the rest of my life a living hell.

"I'm leaving town for a while to clear my head," I told Jeff, my lawyer.

"Now that this last case is over I need to figure out how to get my life

back on track."

"I understand man. Be careful."

"Um. What more can she do to me?" I asked without really expecting

an answer.

Want to know what happens next?

"Saved By The Chase is available on Amazon and Kindle

Unlimited.

Download and start reading today.

Saved By The Chase

AMBW Winter Romance

By Love Journey

OTHER BOOKS BY LOVE JOURNEY

KPOP Promise Series

Remember Tonight

This Love With U

But I Love You Tonight

AMBW Romance

Train My Heart

Live Love Aloha

Beautiful Essence

Janya

I Don't Disappoint

AMBW Sexy Geek Series

Addictive Behavior

A Chance to Love You

AMBW Winter Romance Series

Saved By The Chase

Chased Back To You

AMBW Paranormal

Red Night

Her Wildest Dreams

Her Unexpected Fate

Fated to Love You

ABOUT THE AUTHOR

Love Journey lives a professional life by day and writes exotic, real love, and deep pleasure by night.

She's a brown girl that has been captivated by the world of Korean, Japanese, Chinese, Thai, and Indian dramas, culture, food, and music.

After dipping into her own personal AMBW romance, Love Journey decided to share her hot little fantasies.

THANK YOU

I love my readers!

Thank you for reading this AMBW Romance.

I would like to say thank you to my talented editors and especially to

my sexy Asian muse for inspiring my dreams and flaming my

imagination.

Please join me on my next journey...

CONTACT

I would love to hear from you!

Email:

LoveJourneyBooks@yahoo.com

LoveJourneyBooks@gmail.com

Blog:

AMBW-Love@blogspot.com

Facebook:

www.facebook.com/LoveJourneyBooks

Twitter:

@lovejourneybook

#AMBWLOVE

Remember
TONIGHT
KPOP Promise Series Book I
Love Journey

KPOP Promise Series Book 2

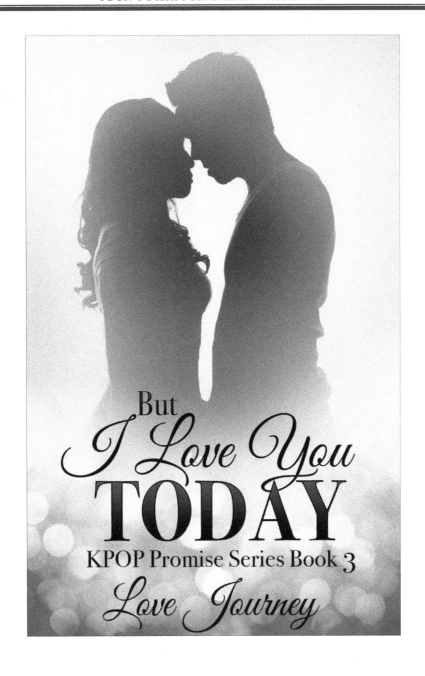

But
I Love You
TODAY
KPOP Promise Series Book 3
Love Journey

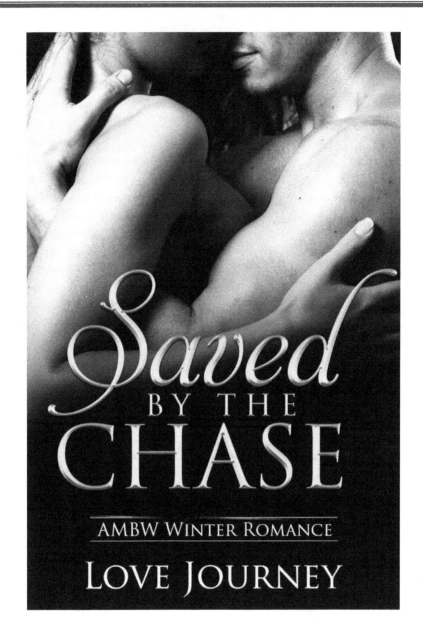

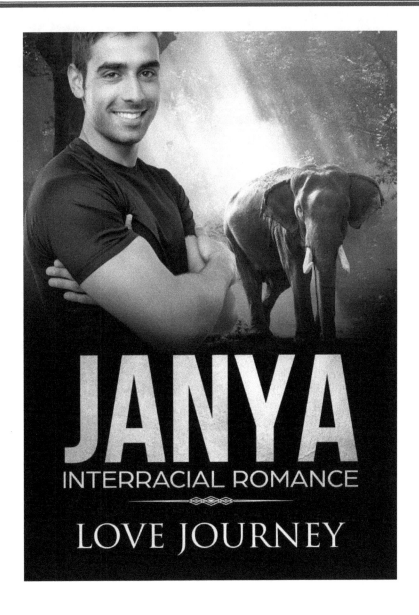

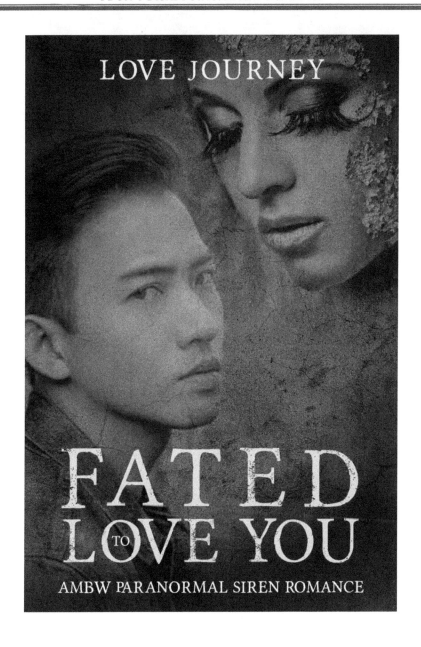

LOVE JOURNEY

FATED
TO
LOVE YOU

AMBW PARANORMAL SIREN ROMANCE

LOVE JOURNEY

Her
UNEXPECTED
FATE

AMBW PARANORMAL SHIFTER ROMANCE

CPSIA information can be obtained
at www.ICGtesting.com
Printed in the USA
LVHW060207280922
729467LV00012B/440